ROB AND THE LOST VILLAGES

ROB AND THE LOST VILLAGES

CHRIS CIACCIO

TABLE OF CONTENTS

FOREWORD

"Hey, wake up, I think my waters have broken," said the woman looking at the sheets in fright. "I can't believe I'm going to have to give birth here." She looked outside the window.

The night was beautiful, and waves gently crashed on the beach beyond. The room was cooler than usual; it had rained a lot in the evening, which was the only time the temperature would ever drop below 18 degrees. The white drapes danced in front of the windows, allowing the brightest star to entertain the room's inhabitants with a stunning light show on the bedroom wall. The soon-to-be-mother slowly rolled over and got to her feet with difficulty as waves of pain tore at her insides. She didn't take anything with her, no pillow or overnight bag, she just dressed, washed up a little, and left the house. A couple of roads, stairs, elevator rides and hallways, a *quick left and a quick right, and she lay with her legs open, pushing life out of her body. After a few hours of agony, the woman had a cute little creature on her breasts.*

What a confusing moment! Every woman feels a mixture of hysterical happiness, absolute fear, confusion, regret, and everything else on that spectrum.

"This is amazing. You're going to raise that baby yourself and this is going to be a great thing for the four of you, don't you worry!" insisted the doctor when he saw the young woman's worried face.

"You're right, it's going to be great, it is not a mistake," lied the young woman. She stared at the little boy for a while and thought of the last time she birthed a beautiful little girl. She had been confused, scared, and insanely happy. However, that first time, she felt no regret, not for a second.

Chapter 1

CHICKEN OR DOG?

It was just another morning in Robat. Robatians were performing their usual chores: fishing in the beautiful lagoon, harvesting the fields at the back of the village by the mountain that towered over Robat, and some were on their way to school. Indarra had been told climbing the mountain was dangerous, as she had been told stories about people who had fallen from the cliffs, become lost, devoured by mysterious creatures, or even sucked in by the rocks themselves for getting too close to the mountain. That was why, like the other 43 inhabitants of Robat, Indarra never walked too close to the mountain that surrounded her little village and plunged into the ocean on both sides of the bay. She was never tempted to get close to it anyway. "I mean, what would be the point!" her dad,

Jerry, would say. "It's not like there's anything beyond it anyway…"

However, it didn't matter, because Indarra didn't care for heights, what she liked was swimming, she would spend hours in the water each day helping her mother, Claire, fishing or just swimming back and forth to the coral reef at the back of the lagoon. Of course, she wouldn't go past the reef because of all the sharks. She hated them and their vicious eyes she couldn't read. Indarra had spotted them when getting too close to the reef, the other side was so packed with them that you could spot at least thirty fins at once just by having a quick glimpse over the reef.

Maggie, one of her teachers and Tom's mother, explained that nature had a way of balancing out. That was how their world appeared – perfect, protected from nothingness by a mountain and by a reef from the sharks. Indarra had always loved Maggie. There was something about her she simply couldn't explain. Also, she liked the fun new activities she came up with and their funky names. Maggie said she came up with the names in her sleep. Indarra told Tom his mother must have had letters in a bag that she picked at random. As much as Indarra hated studying in the morning, she loved spending time with Tom and afternoons were a great time to enjoy everything a place like Robat had to offer such as swimming, running, and ball games that kept the Robatians busy until dawn.

Thanks to the makers in the roundhouse, they had all the tools necessary to produce anything they really needed. The Second Generation was not allowed into the round-house, besides, the burners were there, and that made it difficult to approach. The burners were small, black, square animals that could rotate from wherever they were hanging, mostly off the walls and ceilings. Apparently, they'd jump on you and eat you if you got too close to them. No one had ever seen them do it, and their mouths couldn't be seen, but no one approached them, as the idea of being devoured alive was truly terrifying. The makers had to go through extensive training to gain the burners' trust so they could make it inside the roundhouse safely.

Indarra was getting ready to start her day. She got up, had breakfast of berries and nuts, showered, got dressed in a T-shirt and shorts as always – she always wore the kind with those three stripes – and then walked to school, which was about 200 meters along the beach from her house. She loved the beach. It was a thin strip of sand from where you could see palm trees, banana trees, and the roofs of the Robatian houses, and, of course, there was the roundhouse and the forum. It was fascinating how everyone knew where he or she was supposed to go.

Linda, Monica's mom, was rushing out of her house as usual, as she buttoned her shirt, headed to the boat to go fishing. Indarra could hear the sound of the tools hitting rocks in the fields at the back of Robat where her dad and his coworkers were harvesting in the fields. Indarra was always surprised why her dad, Jerry, spent so much time with Madeleine after work as they already spent a lot of time working together in the fields. Indarra wondered if the First Generation could be friends with one another too. It's true that one day Tom and Indarra would be First Generation themselves and Indarra could not imagine not being friends with Tom anymore.

Indarra spotted Tom walking from the other side of the beach towards the school. Tom was different from other members of the Second Generation. It was something she never talked about with Tom, but a lot of the Second Generation had made fun of him when he was a kid. To the Robatians, it looked like the matter under his skin was softer than all the other Second Generation, and his belly was funny: it was not separated into eight blocks but was just one big block. Somehow, this oddity kept Tom from having any friends as a child, except Indarra, who really didn't care about his belly. Indarra could have had many friends but decided that Tom was enough. The twins were OK too.

"Hi, Tom," said Indarra.

"Hey," replied Tom.

"Crap, I can't believe we have an entire morning of indoor classes with Da Silva."

"He's not so bad," replied Tom.

"Yeah, he's not so bad because you're Maggie's son and he fancies your mom," said Indarra giving Tom a mocking smile.

"No, he does not, don't be ridiculous!" replied Tom faking outrage.

"Alright, alright, I'll pretend I believe that, but that doesn't change anything about the fact that Da Silva is an asshole."

"Language!" said Tom imitating Da Silva's voice.

"A little bitch?"

"Opinionated!" declared Tom. "Yeah, that's what he is."

"Alright, I'm not gonna start criticizing your soon-to-be new daddy."

Tom hit Indarra in the back of her head and they started laughing.

"Alright, hurry, Indarra, it's 8:30 AM and we're gonna be late. You don't wanna make my daddy wait."

They both giggled and made their way to school. The school was a simple one-story building, unlike the houses that had a second floor. The forum, which had a flat roof with tables and chairs, technically only had one floor but the rooftop could be considered the second level. The school was by the beach, on the left side of Robat, and just a large square room with a few additional storage rooms. It comfortably accommodated all 18 of the Second Generation and was very practical. Each student had their own thick metal table and chair on the thick hardwood floors.

Indarra had once held a pretty elaborate presentation about her food habits there; it went for six hours and she'd managed to leave the 'exhibition' up on the class walls for almost two weeks until Tom's mom finally convinced her to take it down. Maggie also explained to her that her message had been heard but her opinion was not something she could force on other people. The twins had complained a lot about sitting for six hours straight. Turk, the most outrageous twin, had actually planned to have his own presentation on a different matter after this event. It was about the makers from the roundhouse. "Seriously, computers seem like a lot of work to make, I mean, how do they even work? Crazy, right? And yet we can't get the roundhouse to give us pillows on our chairs at school?" Turk had said. He complained for a while but didn't have Indarra's willpower so, of course, he never came through, and his sensitive-butt issue was never addressed.

Tom and Indarra sat in the far corner of the school room. Indarra sat close to the window so she could escape Da Silva 's unbearable voice for a second and look at the waves rolling gently on the beach.

"Morning everyone!" said Da Silva sounding detached and without making eye contact with anyone.

Everyone greeted him back, some were more enthusiastic than others were.

"Motivation is ultimately the biggest goal and I need you all to have a goal to study hard. Fishing is not just about killing as many fish as possible. No!" he insisted. "Fish have different mating seasons; some reproduce more and do it faster. The bay is a fragile place and if you kill too many of a species, you might cause their extinction. The same goes for home maintenance and repair. If a branch falls through a roof and the person in charge doesn't fix it properly, you might not see tons of water gushing through the roof into your bathroom as that would be too easy, instead, the water could slowly get into the walls and floors until the house rots from the inside out. Then the only solution will be to tear it down and rebuild it. And believe me, you probably won't be able to. This is why we have put together updated versions of books for every activity needed to keep this place together; you don't have to know it all right away, just know it's there and look through it if you need to.

This went on for a while as Da Silva mentioned many other skills and duties about the different tasks that needed to be accomplished in Robat. Some of the Second Generation were listening, but most of them had zoned out five minutes in. Indarra was one of them, but she'd sometimes refocus when she heard something interesting or mostly something off or silly, then, she'd roll her eyes, and look back out of the window where it seemed to promise of a brighter afternoon. Da Silva spoke of water supply and a gush at the bottom of the mountain from which water from underground caves came, apparently from rainfall absorbed by the mountain. He showed a map, which displayed the layout of pipes that ran from the spring underground to each house. There was also a wheel for hydroelectricity and another map that showed the cables connected to homes. The small stream of water then disappeared in the mountain behind the forum. Da Silva then started talking about fixing fridges after mentioning many other appliances. Indarra decided to interrupt loud enough she would be clearly heard by everyone. Da Silva was extremely annoyed at Indarra's interruption but he had no choice but to listen to what she had to say.

"I think it's cool that we learn how to fix some of those things. I get that some of us will have to do it, but I feel like we're spending a lot of energy learning obvious things that most of us know perfectly like how to grow food, fish, and fix toilet pipes," said Indarra sounding a little condescending of Da Silva's teaching methods. "On the other hand, how were fridges invented? How are they made? How do they work? I mean, honestly, it's one of those things that we all take from granted, like dishwashers, I'm glad they're there and I'm glad they work, the same way I'm happy the sun rises every morning to light the village and I'm glad it sets every night so I can sleep in the dark. The only difference is that I think the sun should remain pretty autonomous. What if a fridge becomes unfixable? How do we make one?"

"You see, my dear Indarra, this is why I'm a trainer and you're only a below average Second Generation. I pass on the knowledge needed and inform you of the tools that can help you keep Robat a great place, while you interrupt, wasting everyone's time with silly questions just to put yourself in the spotlight. But let me explain to you why you don't need to learn how those things were made; my generation and the previous ones have built an extraordinary place and none of these appliances is even remotely close to being beyond repair. A new fridge might not need to be made for one or two generations, so why waste our time with it? If needed, the next generations will find information about it on the computer or in books."

Da Silva was extremely proud of himself for leaving Indarra speechless. It would probably be the highlight of his week. He pretended to be modest about his victory and went on. "Who can tell me how long a person can live?" asked Da Silva.

"Fifty to 55 years," answered Deborah, an insufferable little know-it-all who was clearly in Da Silva's good favor.

Indarra rolled her eyes and she and Tom started giggling.

"Anything interesting you'd like to share with us, Indarra?" asked Da Silva defiantly.

"No nothing, Da Silva."

"If you're laughing in class, I'm guessing you have nothing to learn about our life cycle here on Robat, so it will surely be easy for you to write a paper on it and give it to me tomorrow," Da Silva said all this without making eye contact with Indarra. It was as if he considered her a useless creature that should not be acknowledged. "Class dismissed. Head to the forum for lunch and to the peer at one to have your afternoon class with Maggie. That's it!" he added, making it clear no one was to speak to him afterward.

"So, we were both laughing but I'm the one who ends up with the assignment and you still don't think there's something fishy about that?" Indarra asked Tom as they rushed out of the classroom.

"It could be anything, maybe it's my charming personality, or maybe he has a crush on me!" said Tom.

"That's crazy, it would be intergenerational," said Indarra as if this was the strangest thing she had ever heard.

"Is that unheard of?"

"I don't know! Hmmm, could you ask your mom? You think she'd tell you?"

"I guess . . ."

Lunch was perfectly orchestrated in Robat, like everything in Robat to be honest. Every day at noon, everyone left their jobs and the First Generation walked back from school, the roundhouse, the ocean, or the fields. The forum staff had everything ready for lunch at 12 sharp and joined the rest of the community to eat on the roof if the weather allowed it. It could rain very heavily in Robat, but the weather was generally very pleasant. Across from Tom and Indarra were the twins, Turk and Ross.

"Hey, Tom, hey, Indarra," said Turk. He and Ross were what you'd call the entertainment in Robat.

"Soooooo, got yourself a little fun for the evening, Indarra," said Ross.

"Looks like it," said Indarra looking annoyed. "We have a whole theory about why I get victimized while Tom seems to be Da Silva's little protégé. We're still deciding if it's his intergenerational love for Tom."

"Ew," interjected Ross.

"I know, right?" said Indarra really satisfied with herself. "Or, and I think this is less fun but more plausible, Da Silva's love for the oh-so-beautiful Maggie, his future wife, and Tom's soon-to-be new daddy." She looked around taking in everyone's amused face. "Wait, I change my mind, that one's even better!" she finally added.

"Nooooo," shouted Turk, "that was my plan. I wanted to be your new daddy!"

Tom was clearly losing control of the situation.

"I agree," said Ross viciously. "I'd like a taste of that First Generation."

"It's my mom, it's gross," said Tom stating the obvious.

"Well, either way, there's something there and Da Silva clearly isn't gonna go for me any time soon," said Indarra faking being hurt.

"Jealous!" said Tom poking Indarra in the stomach. They started laughing.

"How's your nothing sandwich?" asked Ross.

"What?" asked Turk not understanding what Ross was talking about.

"Yeah . . . Indarra doesn't eat small living things remember? She is fighting for the chicken sandwich and beans to be replaced with dog sandwich and eggplant," said Tom rolling his eyes.

"Turk!" said Indarra offended, "mock me all you want, but do you know how many beans are needed to feed one person? Well, about 27 for a side dish. Do you know how many eggplants need to be sacrificed? Huh you know, huh?!"

Tom felt a little scared by her crazy eyes.

"Keep it together woman and eat your bread and mayo with your side of fresh air," said Ross laughing. "I get it! What's the dog to chick ratio?"

"Glad you asked," and she smiled, satisfied. "What ratio? A chicken feeds three, a dog feeds 17. There! You have it, so next time I'll expect you to have a nothing sandwich with me instead of all of this nonsense."

"Oh, yeah, that's nonsense alright," mocked Ross.

"You're just saying that because you think that chickens are cute," said Tom dismissing her opinion, which she did not appreciate.

"Alright, I guess chickens are not that small. I'll meet everyone half-way by removing it from my list of complaints, but no more beans OK?"

"She is so weak," exclaimed Ross. "Girl, that hunger strike did not last long!"

"Shut up, Ross!" screamed Indarra throwing her spoon at him.

"What's this afternoon?" asked Turk bored by the conversation.

"Some new sport my mom invented. I think there was 'bang' in the word; it's probably some water sport again."

Chapter 2

INTERGENERATIONNATING

"A water sport? Well done, one block!" mocked Ross. "Oh, shut your dumb face, Ross!" said Indarra in indignation, so angry her voice almost sounded like she was crying.

Tom laughed and kinda waved it away as if he thought it was funny and actually didn't care but Indarra could tell he was bothered and that the mockery, though friendly from them, had been sometimes cruel and there was no way he could have gotten over it all.

As it turned out, the sport didn't sound like 'bang' at all and neither was it a water sport, but everyone enjoyed the afternoon much more than they had enjoyed their morning in Da Silva's company. The only one who didn't enjoy herself was Deborah who received no favors from Maggie. It was not that Maggie treated her badly, in fact, she was treated fairly, which wasn't what she was used to from Da Silva.

Tom and Indarra started playing against one another until she obviously beat him, then they swapped with the twins. Indarra beat Ross but lost to Turk. Ross kept losing the small white ball, which was really hard to find on the white sand.

The afternoon ended with an actual water ball sport at which Indarra was unbeatable. Turk, who was probably as competitive as Indarra, was soon red in the face over her prowess. As he didn't exactly lose, she was just better, they agreed to say they both won. Yes, alright, I think we all know she won, they both knew it...

"You all played very well," interrupted Maggie, "but you all need to work on your underwater abilities. You don't need it for anything we do yet in Robat but it's a great skill to acquire, Indarra, this bit will interest you most," and she looked at Indarra with persistence. "On the west side of our beautiful reef, at the very bottom, there's a small cave where the best fish hide. Very few people can get there because it's very deep but it's worth the struggle as this is where Robat gets its biggest fish!"

After a long day, they all returned to their houses to shower and get ready for the evening festivities of dinner with the whole community. Jerry had already showered and was in the living room when Claire went to get ready – she always finished work a little later. Indarra was in her own bathroom getting rid of the salt from the sea. They all gathered downstairs a bit later and started sharing their experiences of the day.

"He did what?" asked Claire of Jerry. Indarra was too far away to hear. "How about you honey?" asked Claire when she noticed she was downstairs too, "did you have a nice day?"

"I got extra work from Da Silva, the afternoon was fun though."

"What did you do to get the extra work?" asked her dad concerned.

"Nothing! I simply dared to giggle for a second, very quietly with Tom, because what's her face was being obnoxious."

"What's the assignment?" asked Claire.

"The cycle of life."

"It's unfair and useless and you have better things to do than writing this piece of garbage. I'll have it ready for you in 15 minutes, so you can copy it in the morning in your handwriting. Cycle of my ass!" she hissed walking towards the console. "Honey, please read it once in case you get quizzed by this man about it, OK? We'd get in trouble if it were too obvious you didn't write it, so read it, won't you?" Her tone meant 'you'd better!'

"Of course, Mom."

Indarra gazed at the sun setting over the ocean from the chair outside of the house as Claire worked on Indarra's assignment. A star that always flashed brightly above the water became brighter every second the sky grew darker.

"Should we get going?" asked Jerry with more intensity than he probably meant.

"It depends!" said Indarra defiantly, "have you been murdering life stock that could feed a tenth of a toddler today?"

"No, I believe it's beef and potato stew tonight, so. . ." smirked Jerry.

By the time they made it up to the forum's rooftop, the sun had almost set and the bright star had lit the entire bay like a searchlight making it impossible to even see the surf break on the coral reef.

"Is she breathing?" asked Ross with false concern as Indarra stuffed her face with potato beef stew.

"A commitment to a noble cause requires discipline and is often challenging!" declared Indarra proudly. "Tom, did you ask your mom about the intergenerational thing?" she queried in between mouthfuls.

"Yeah, I did. She froze for a second and seemed to have to think about it a lot longer as it clearly was not a question she expected," said Tom.

"Come again?" asked Ross puzzled.

"Keep up! you know Da Silva is weirdly nice to me and Indarra was wondering whether he was into me or my mom and we wondered if there were any records of inter-generational relationships and whether we find it gross or not," said Tom flatly.

"Well, it depends," Turk was smirking.

"On?" asked Tom with little interest.

"Whether I'm intergenerationating with your mother or some old fart!" screamed Turk with Maggie only two tables away.

They were all laughing but Tom stopped them by saying loudly, "Anyway! About that intergenerational thing, she did not seem to know what to say. She said she had never wondered about it and wasn't sure how to feel about it but that adults are free to do whatever they want. She asked me why I asked though and I told her Turk was only into First Generation and was wondering whether it was fine or not . . . She just nodded and didn't seem surprised at all."

Turk threw his beef at Tom while Indarra watched in exasperation but didn't say anything.

"Anyway, problem solved, Turk can get fossils," Tom said and they all laughed, even Turk.

After dinner, the whole crew headed back to their homes for the night while the forum staff cleaned up the place and got things ready for the next day.

Breakfast was a fast event in Robat. Every night, bags of food were given to the Robatians on their way home from dinner with simple nutritious things in it. There was no warm food or communal gathering as there was no time for that, so Indarra often ate breakfast in the bathroom while getting ready.

The following morning in class, Professor Log taught a theoretical survival class that was adapted to life in Robat. However, for Robatians who grew up in Robat the skills were already known and obvious to them. The first lesson was about self-defense against monkeys. Monkeys were known to be vicious but having a lesson about them seemed pointless as everyone in Robat knew that to protect themselves you just threw their feces back at them!

"Log is totally losing it," stated Ross as he walked out of the classroom after four hours of boredom. "I mean, monkeys! What's next? How to avoid apples falling from trees and how to use shower gel?"

"I know," said Turk while walking up Main Street to the forum. The street was shaded by palm trees to keep the Robatians cool from the burning sun, or, as it had suddenly started raining, keep them dry for a few minutes. "First, we had that stupid class yesterday about plumbing and that other one in which your mother taught us about first aid treatment for shark bites. I mean, who needs this?"

"Maybe people who get turtle bites?" asked Ross, poking Indarra with his elbow, expecting laughter and an audience to his amazing joke.

She gave him a kind smile, a forced one, as it did not deserve much more to be honest. "You guys don't get it," said Indarra. "They're training us for the takeover."

"What?" asked Tom who had literally just arrived from the outside.

At the forum, they stayed downstairs as it was still raining. They all grabbed a tray, cutlery, and glasses. The forum was a little busy since the floor had to fit the kitchen, the serving area, and all the tables and chairs while the roof, being the same size, only had to accommodate the tables and chairs. The forum spaces could be used for many other reasons like village meetings and celebrations, but above all, it was used for shelter when that huge wave had hit them when they were about 12 years old. On that day, the sea had vanished initially and then hit really hard. Luckily, Jerry had seen the wave while he was fishing and had time to raise the alarm.

"Morning, Timber, spoiling us again today?" asked Turk sarcastically.

"Why don't you shut that big mouth of yours," said the man while handing a plate of food to Ross.

"Cruel," whispered Turk with a smirk.

"Hey, Indarra, how's your father?" asked Timber.

"Great thanks, he is great, thanks for asking," she answered politely. "What's on the menu today?" she asked all business-like.

"Baked flounder and sautéed zucchini," declared Timber with pride.

"Hmm, I guess I can have it," said Indarra while interrogating her friends with her eyes, somehow asking for their approval to eat lunch.

"I would skip that one," said Ross with fake concern, "I'm not sure a flounder feeds more than 12 . . ." He looked at his brother as if wanting him to add his personal touch to her torture.

"You are right, Ross, thank you!" almost cried Indarra in real concern, "I'll only have the zucchini, I mean," her voice trailed off on the last word, "for a vegetable, it's pretty big," she said, not entirely convinced, but scared to see her only source of food taken away from her.

"My poor girl, you do realize we cook and prepare food for each person here, so if you don' eat it, I'll just throw it away," said Timber in a manner that was half-sorry half mocking.

"Well, that's just silly," said Indarra recovering her confidence. "Someone could eat it tomorrow and you could make one less of the other dish then." It was one more lost battle for Indarra.

After this little incident, they took their seats close to the window where they could still see the sea. The room was packed and everyone had to be loud to be heard.

"Take over!" exclaimed Tom returning to what he had overheard when he arrived. "That's just impossible; take over isn't for at least another two years so why would they train us now?"

"Yeah, I thought it was weird," said Indarra. "We're supposed to be trained for takeover half a year before it happens. I mean they can teach us some related stuff about it, but nothing that specific and they're somehow not acknowledging that this is what they're doing."

"Have your parents ever told you about their own take-over?" asked Tom.

"Not really," said Ross. "They said it was fun and we would have the place to ourselves, but nothing specific. To be honest, I never thought about it much."

"Well, either way, this is not conforming with the procedure," said Indarra, her mouth full of zucchini. "Remember that class about reproduction and now the life cycles which we seem to be looking at with more persistence. I just find it odd."

"I just don't get how it . . . how does it work? I mean, do we suddenly take charge? Do they just grow old and die in the years to come and we reproduce and it starts all over again? That's just odd; they seem so lively so how can they be so close to death?" asked Turk, not looking his usual careless self.

"We deteriorate fast, that's just how it works, and we will learn more about it during takeover training. Anyway it's not like takeover just happens; there's a shift in management from one generation to the next but they'll still be around a couple years till they all die," said Indarra. "I mean, I don't know, we're just starting to learn about that. None of us had even heard of a takeover until recently so . . . I'm just really excited about career prospects – that's the main part of the takeover – as we will all choose a career path and we'll be trained to take over that position. They seem to have a whole thing about the builders though like they don't want us to take over that part, but then the current builders will die so I just don't get how this can possibly work . . . I think I wanna specialize in underwater fishing, how fun would it be? What will you guys go for?"

"I wanna be a teacher," said Turk. "So I can cancel class every day and finally make this place fun!"

"Don't be ridiculous!" snapped Indarra, "you can't cancel class, and you'd need to really improve your grades, only highly trustworthy Second Generations can aspire to professorial positions."

"Snore!" teased Ross. "Indarra! Why? Why spoil our meal?" laughed Ross once again looking at his brother and expecting back up. "Can't you just let us enjoy our fantasy? Either way, I know what I'm worth. I might not be a great reader or anything of that sort, but I sure can cook! But being reminded by a friend that my intellectual capacities are limited when it already is a sore spot really saddens me." Ross started playing with his napkin looking down and away from Indarra for dramatic effect, then he looked up at his brother and smiled devilishly knowing he had left Indarra confused and embarrassed.

Indarra quickly recovered and added, "Tom, you should be a teacher! You're super smart, capable, organized, and there's no reason why you couldn't make it."

"I guess . . ." Tom sounded bored. "I haven't really thought about it. I guess working in the fields would be quieter and more relaxing as I'm not sure I'm good enough with people."

"Yes, well, each and every job is important; whatever makes you comfortable, Tom. I would just hate to see your talent go to waste just because you don't realize your worth, and," she added looking at the twins, "you don't want that job to fall in the hands of people like Turk or our future Second Generation will become absolute idiots!"

Indarra awoke to a usual warm and sunny Robat morning. Monkeys were dangling from the branches outside throwing poop at anyone who would look at them for too long, and the fish were starting to swim deeper to avoid the heat of the sun. The only thing that was slightly unusual was the behavior of Indarra's parents that morning.

"Honey, you take good care. You are sure you won't be cold like this?" Claire was trying to cover Indarra's arms with her shirt, which was useless unless she managed to stretch the sleeves below her elbows.

"Mom! It's 29 degrees outside and I'm wearing what I always wear."

"Of course, hun, well, I believe if you just trust your instincts you'll be fine, OK?"

"Sure, Mom, I'll trust my instincts about my outfit, thanks." She turned to her father who was busy doing something on the other side of the room. "Dad! What's wrong with Mom? What's wrong with you? Why do you look like you just saw a ghost?"

"Nothing, hun, we just love you so much!"

"OK, I love you too you weirdoes who stole my parent's bodies." She pretended to be amused by the situation but was starting to get worried.

Chapter 3

WE'RE IN CHARGE

The morning class was again very intense and neither Tom, Indarra, Turk or Ross had a second to talk to one another.

"Crap, my mom cried at breakfast," exclaimed Tom while digging into his food at lunchtime in the forum.

"What? Why?" asked Indarra.

"I don't know, you?"

"Well, my parents didn't cry but they've been acting like absolute lunatics."

"No I mean my mom was bugging me about you. She was going on about how lucky she was to have met your dad and that regardless of the fact that our relationship was friendly and not romantic it didn't make a bit of a difference and that, when you love somebody you should stay by their side and follow them. Follow them? Where would

I follow you? That's just weird! Why would I start pacing behind you like a stalker?"

"Keep your voice down, your mom is looking at us," ordered Indarra.

Maggie got up from her chair leaving a couple of the First Generation behind her and walked to Tom and Indarra's table, "Here is your geology essay from Log. He asked me to hand them back to you as he wants you to read the corrections before his class tomorrow." Then, she looked at Indarra with an odd intensity and said, "It looks like you need to work on those rocks!"

"What!" asked Indarra softly, intimidated by this charismatic woman.

"You didn't do great at this test; you need to work on it, Indarra."

Indarra looked at her test and was about to say something but stopped herself when she saw the look in Maggie's eyes.

"Seriously, what happened? You're usually great at geology. How did you manage to get a bad grade? Give me it!" said Tom as he tried to reach for the test.

Indarra was faster than him and tossed it in her pocket. The twins arrived a minute later and sat with Tom and Indarra who told them all about their weird morning.

"Do you think this has something to do with Tom having an affair with his mother's lover?" sniggered Turk.

Tom put his hands to his ears and pretended to dry heave. "OMG, this sick mind of yours!"

Everyone laughed, even Indarra.

Ross looked at his brother in a way that meant, 'that joke was good, you have my full respect brother and then said', "Has every First Generation been weird to their kids?"

"You can say that. We need to figure out what's going on but we can't ask because they will lie, however, they can't figure out what we are up to," said Indarra.

"Do you guys think it could be because they found out that the final test is going to be a bitch this year and that they feel pity and wanna prepare us or something? Maybe it's going to be physically excruciating and they feel terrible?" said Turk.

Indarra considered it for a moment and replied, "That's an interesting idea, Turk, and we will sure keep it in mind in our brainstorming! However, I don't think that would explain all of their behavior."

Ross tried it too, but it didn't satisfy Indarra either, "Could it be that the huge wave we had when we were younger is about to hit us again? Maybe we're all going to die because the one coming now is even bigger, so they're saying goodbye but don't wanna tell us because what would be the point? So, they're trying to pretend like our life is going to go on but failing miserably and behaving like lunatics?"

This explanation didn't satisfy Indarra either.

"I overheard Dad speak of food reserves, he seemed worried. I didn't give it much importance at first but now I'm wondering! Are we running out of food? Could that be it? And we're all gonna die or something and they feel terrible and wanna make us notice it as late as possible," gasped Turk.

"Again, very interesting and smart ideas," continued Indarra, "but that doesn't explain why Tom's mom wants him to follow me and the advice from my parents. If we were all gonna die, why would they bother giving us tips for the future? You know? I feel like if a huge wave or hunger was lurking from the corner, they wouldn't be acting this way at all. Instead, they would be like, 'no school, you kids get an early vacation and let's have a feast on the beach!' Right?" Indarra looked at the sky and declared. "OK, let's get through the day, focus on our afternoon, try to have a good time, have dinner, get to bed early, and how about we meet an hour earlier tomorrow morning in front of the silo. That way we can think about it together. That's the only time we can really be alone and by then we will probably have figured out a few more things."

Throughout the evening, all four of them only had one thing in mind, discovering what was going on. Indarra knew something bad was going to happen and thought that their parents were trying to protect them by not telling them the truth, but she thought keeping them in the dark could also put them in danger.

Goodnights were even weirder than the good-mornings. Jerry's eyes were red and puffy as if he had cried and Claire was just dead silent and looked unable to focus on anything. Her hands kept shaking while she tried to fix the cabinet knob that had been loose for months and to which she had given no interest but somehow tonight she couldn't sleep unless the knob was fixed.

Indarra woke up twice that night, first to the noise of her parents speaking, which was really unusual – they almost seemed to be fighting even though she couldn't hear what they were saying. The second time, she woke up to what she thought was a bang but fell right back asleep.

She woke up two hours earlier than usual, which meant she still had an hour to spare since the four of them were only meeting an hour earlier than school time. She stayed in bed for a bit; the intense silence in the house filled her with calm and certainty that the future would be fine and nothing terrible would happen. She had breakfast at the kitchen table for once instead of the bathroom since she had more time than usual. She found Log's essay that was handed back by Maggie the day before and thought of her. She'd always had a very special relationship with Maggie. She couldn't explain why, being from different generations, families, and as her teacher, it was not as if they could be casual with each other, but they just had that respect for one another and Maggie, although distant and formal always had this warm and caring vibe towards her. Indarra would often catch Maggie looking at her, even for a second, in a way she never understood as it looked protective and yet so furtive.

It was now time to head to the silo. The sun had not yet made its way over the horizon, but you could make out that kind of glow you get an hour before the sun comes out. The big star, which was always shining on the horizon, seemed to have moved a bit, not drastically but it was always perfectly in front of her house and now seemed to be slightly off to the right. It made her feel uneasy, as if this star was the last stable thing they'd had until it moved.

Indarra walked along the beach, staring at the big star from time to time. She realized that without being aware of it, she had seen it so consistently her whole life that she somehow knew where it was supposed to be wherever she was standing in the bay and it now looked wrong from wherever she was standing that morning. She made a right on Main Street, walked past the forum, made a left at the back of the village, walked past the barn, and finally reached the silo where Tom was waiting. The twins were late and had probably slept in. Tom looked worried and was pacing. He didn't seem to have noticed that Indarra was only eight meters away from him now and actually got startled when she touched his shoulder to greet him.

"Somebody seems lost in his thoughts this morning," she said.

"Oh, hi, Indarra, it's you!"

"Who did you expect to find at this hour by the silo?"

"We need to be quiet. I think my mother is out here, we could get in trouble." Tom looked around him nervously.

"What? What makes you say that?"

"My mom can't sleep with the lights off. She always has her nightlight on, always. I can see it under the door, but today, nothing, the light was off, so she must be out here, she must know we're up to something and decided to catch us red-handed."

"That's ridiculous. Are you sure she didn't go to the bathroom, got over her fear, or the light bulb just died? There could be a million reasons it's not on. No one heard us plan this and I can't picture your mom doing something like this, she would have just told you she knew and would have asked what you were up to directly. She's not sneaky like this."

"You must be right. Let's keep our voices down anyway and our eyes open even if my mom has permanently settled in the bathroom at night and decided it would be a secure place to sleep in the dark. . . You idiot!" Tom said and winked.

Indarra opened her mouth in false indignation and laughed as the twins made a turn to the left from Main Street.

Ross spoke first, "So kiddos, any thoughts on the weirdness?"

"I don't know, I can't really think of anything. I think we should pay attention in class," said Tom.

"For a change!" Indarra added looking at the twins.

They went on debating for an hour and tried to work through the twins' stupid ideas such as Da Silva and Maggie's wedding to absolute craziness such as an imminent giant crab attack.

"Tom thinks his mother is searching for us, she is not in her room," said Indarra.

"I know what's happening," Turk said. "I've seen her blush while looking at me these past few days. That's what's going on and that's why she is out of bed. I must go back to bed, she's searching for me so she can get in my room and we can—"

Loud voices and screams drowned out Turk's final comment.

"Did you hear that?" whispered Tom.

"Of course we did," said Indarra. "Let's go see what's happening. It's coming from the beach. We have to act casual as we have no reason to be coming from the back of the village at this hour so let's go quietly and try to hide, we don't want your mother or anyone else to see us."

They made a right on Main Street and by the time they made it to the forum, they were half-way to the beach with only 200 meters to go. The whole idea of trying to be discreet soon seemed useless considering the chaos and confusion they witnessed on the beach. All the Second Generations were running, screaming, and banging at everyone's door shouting. The first voice they made out was Julie's as she ran along the beach calling for her parents. Soon everyone realized they were all doing the same thing: going from one house to the next asking for their parents. The four of them just stood there watching the scene unravel before their eyes knowing exactly what was happening as if they had known all along but couldn't face it so hadn't even come up with the idea. They didn't speak or look at each other. They didn't run to their houses or call for their parents since they already knew it would be pointless. The First Generation had vanished.

After what seemed like hours, but probably was less than 10 minutes, the hysteria quietened down and small groups formed, some by the water and others on house patios. A few sat by themselves and several were still frenetically searching for their parents. *If I remember correctly, Indarra told me that some just stayed in their houses for hours and wouldn't come out. It must have been strange to see people in their late 20s screaming for their parents like children, but I guess even if we become more independent, we'll always be someone's child. This place also separated me from my family so I know what it feels like.*

Turk turned to his friends first. "What now?"

"How can they be gone?" stuttered Tom. "Why? You think they died? Or they left us? Where would they go? Did they go to the sharks and got eaten alive? Did they go up the mountain and die? Why would they do that? I mean the transition isn't happening now. Maybe they're coming back or—"

Indarra put a finger to his lips. "Calm down, Tom. Breathe, relax, but accept the truth, I'm sorry to tell you that, but I don't think they're coming back."

"Don't say that, how can they not come back?" mumbled a panicked Ross. "None of this makes sense, it's just ridiculous."

"Listen all of you, we shouldn't panic. We need to stay calm and use our brains to figure things out. We will find out what happened, but the reality is they're gone and they're not coming back. It all adds up – remember how they began preparing us for transition this early, their sadness, and weird behavior. And, Tom, your mother out of bed . . . They knew they wouldn't be part of the equation anymore for whatever reason, but they also knew we would remain part of the equation and that's exactly why they kept on living as if things would continue on Robat, because things will continue. We will search and find out what happened, but first, we have to accept that the transition has happened and that we're in charge."

"Only there was no transition. We're supposed to have our jobs assigned and we should be trained properly for them. It's going to be chaos. Why would anyone agree to take care of the cleaning of the forum when they haven't been nominated by the First Generation?" said Turk in alarm.

"Wow, for someone who's usually so chilled and carefree, you put a lot of thought into this and seem to know a lot about the transition! And now you're blushing," added Tom to destabilize Turk even more. It probably worked.

"I'm not blushing. I don't really care, I'm just stating the obvious."

I remember the first thing Turk ever said to me: 'Barbecue has never really been my thing as it's too sweet; I'm more of a Hollandaise kinda guy.' He was referring to my burns.

Indarra, who I had met a few hours before, looked at him stupefied. I immediately understood that he was more of a 'too soon' kinda guy than Hollandaise. He had blushed that time too, realizing how everyone was shocked by what he had just said. This clumsiness of his is something I have of course learned to love, but it took some time!

Lunch never happened, not because no one knew how to work their way around the kitchen or by lack of organization, but no one thought about eating till the sun started setting over Robat. And that's how the new First Generation spent their first post-transition day. Somehow, it could have been worse but they stopped panicking, had normal and calm conversations, and tried to figure everything out.

⊟⊨

I wanna take you away from Robat for a short moment and, well . . . straight into my slightly bigger town. Did you ever have anyone in your life who felt it was their job to make you do things, even if you were already doing so much more than they do? These kinds of people feel entitled to this privilege for different stupid reasons; they're older, they own a penis, or they believe their social status not only allows them but actually burdens them with this task. Whatever it is, they enjoy belittling you by telling you to do something you already have done or will do or that they can and should do themselves! Please meet Jack!

"If you don't like their songs then you probably don't understand them, or you just don't have the right sensibility or any sensibility at all," interjected the boy.

"But it's just noise! That's not music! What's with all the screaming?" asked Jack.

"They're in pain! That's what it is, that's the message they're trying to convey, a message not everyone can receive apparently . . . Just have some more cake!"

The music enthusiast had made the food along with a few people from the group while Jack sat on his ass. Everyone participated and had a great time and yet, Jack still asked the music enthusiast to refill someone's cup, while comfortably seated in his armchair like a king. Do we hate Jack? No, because aside from that, he is a great guy, but it is annoying to a point where it makes you wanna grab that person and shake it out of them. That's it, back to Robat!

<hr/>

Tom, who was usually not much of a leader and even left out by his peers when he was younger, found it easy to take charge and people quickly respected him and listened.

The four of them were the perfect leadership combination; the twins were popular because of their humor and positivity, Indarra was smart, and Tom was the son of the most respected former First Generation on Robat. There never was a leader on Robat, not an official one that Robatians knew of at least, and tasks and roles were assigned at transition. Somehow it worked and that is what happened over the course of the first day. Somehow, the fishers' kids naturally went fishing, the cooks' kids made their way into the kitchen, and the farmers' kids started harvesting. There were only a few jobs not taken. These included the makers from the roundhouse because no one had access, the cleaners as no one wanted to, the doctor as the doctor's kid didn't have anything to do since he didn't know how, and no one was sick plus the doctor worked in the roundhouse too – well, only for surgeries, minor problems were dealt with at the forum. They would put you out in your bed, take you to the roundhouse and you'd wake up in your bed. That's how Indarra got her appendectomy.

Tom helped out whoever seemed a bit lost. Having had a teacher for a mother, he had learned a lot in many different fields, so somehow, he could answer people's questions about most jobs. By the time the sun set, everyone gathered for dinner. The room seemed empty now that almost two-thirds of the population had gone. The population had dropped from 43 to 16.

Deborah seemed absolutely lost and her friend Melissa wasn't doing much better. Deborah's parents had both worked in the fields and even SHE had helped a bit today back there, although it was not without complaining and maybe not as hard as the rest of the new First Generation. She had always hated Tom because his mother was respected, so loved by everyone, and was someone she felt her parents were not. Though she was not bad looking, she had that expression on her pale face that made her very unattractive. Her hair was coal black and her features were hard and angular. She looked a lot older than any-one else of her generation even though they were all about 25. Melissa had a long, angular horse face and was really tall. Her mom was the doctor of Robat and nicer than her daughter but had never been really outgoing.

"Can you believe the fat one over there?" bellowed Deborah. "Who does he think he is? Giving out orders to everyone like he's the boss or something, just because his dumb mother was a teacher. I miss Da Silva."

"I don't know," started Melissa with that naive voice of hers. "I mean we need to eat and all and maybe his mother wasn't so bad. She was always nice to me."

"Shut up you idiot, if they think I won't—"

The sound of Ross tripping on the leg of a chair interrupted Deborah. As he fell, the food on his tray splattered everywhere. Everyone laughed, including Ross who, even though he was a bit embarrassed, didn't appear to be. The Robatians needed a laugh and whether it was on purpose or not, Ross had done his job in keeping up their morale. It also served to break the conversation between Deborah and Melissa so Indarra didn't get to hear the rest of it. The twins had been working the kitchen and Indarra got Turk's tray while he finished up. It turns out they could cook a pretty decent dinner and had even considered Indarra's by serving no chicken or beans on the menu that day but a delicious lamb stew, and they ate it all. It might have been because they had skipped a meal, or because they had experienced an array of emotions that day, but everyone ate their whole plate and went straight to bed.

"Guys!" said Ross as he cleaned up the forum – the twins took their new job seriously and wouldn't let Tom and Indarra help, well, not until they insisted just a little. "Can you believe today?"

"I know, it's crazy, I can't even wrap my mind around it yet. Is it worse than what we expected?" asked Tom as he scratched his head and tried to figure out how he felt about it.

"Really, this was doomed to happen at some point anyway, only it was supposed to be later, and we were supposed to be prepared and . . . wait!" Indarra suddenly stopped put a hand to her chin and frowned. "How did they dispose of the bodies?"

"The crazy lady says what?" joked Turk.

"I think it was the sharks," Tom said. "My mom told me about it vaguely one day. I guess that would make sense and it's the reason why they stick around . . ."

"Crazy fatty says what?"

Indarra kicked Turk in the leg and said, "I meant when the First Generation dies! I was wondering how they disposed of the bodies."

"The sharks wait for a whole generation? That seems like a lot of waiting." Ross seemed skeptical. "Indarra, you should start eating them; they're really big!"

"Ha, ha, ha," Indarra insisted on each 'ha' and shook her head. "You're so funny, Ross, how about I eat you?"

"That meat is nasty, you'd get sick," joked his brother.

"We're twins, you idiot!" Ross said. "We'd taste the same."

"Congrats on the food, kids, that was really good." Indarra decided to put an end to the silliness. After all, they had more important things to talk about.

"Thanks, we like the job, it has short hours, and we get to make a point through food – if we don't like you or you've done something to us, you get small quantities and bad food. It's like a real weapon when you know how to use it."

"Ross, you're not supposed to serve different things to people just because you hold a grudge against them, that's just not right."

"That's why we won't tell you about it, you buzz kill! Keep going and you're having mussels for lunch tomorrow, Indarra."

"I can't bring myself to go to that house alone tonight, it's just so weird. I've never slept in a house by myself," sighed Tom.

"Me neither, wanna stay at mine? I have an extra room now," said Indarra.

"Why don't you guys stay with us? We have three bedrooms: Turk and I can share a room and you'll get one room each."

"Thanks, guys, I think that's a fantastic idea. We need to stick together now and I don't think that there's any kind of danger, but better be safe than sorry and err . . . no."

"What's wrong now? Don't just say err!" said Tom.

"I don't know, I'm probably wrong but when I walked to the silo this morning, an hour before the whole confusion here and the screaming, well, I think I heard something, like a muffled scream or voice."

"Maybe it was someone talking in their sleep or something," said Turk.

"Right, that's what I first thought, but then, I don't know. It came from deeper, further."

"What do you mean deeper? Like underground?" asked Tom.

"I don't know, just further, like, if you stand on the beach, right?" Indarra pointed at the beach with her left hand. "And I stand at the back of the field, that's as far apart as we can be unless maybe you're by the coral reef but even then, if you screamed, I'd hear a scream, I could maybe almost make up words if you screamed loud enough and the wind was in the right direction, OK? It was super quiet and if someone were speaking from that distance, I would have heard a muffled voice. Well, I heard a muffled scream. That's it."

"How do you know it was a muffled scream since you've never heard a muffled scream?" asked Ross.

"Well, Ross! I've heard screams before, I've heard muffled voices before, so if I put those together, I get a muffled scream and I think that this is what I heard." She hesitated for a moment and said. "Guys, I think they're up in the mountain."

"What? Why would they go there? Do you think that's how they dispose of bodies? That would mean transition actually is more violent than we've been told and that the First Generation just marches up to the mountain to be cruelly devoured? That's ridiculous," snapped Tom.

"Is it though? I mean it would make sense if you think of the atmosphere if we knew they would die this way. The goodbyes would just be terrible. Could you picture us throwing our parents to the sharks? Bodies have to go some-where and we certainly can't take them to the mountain."

"I don't know, Indarra, why do they have to die altogether?"

"Well, that just how it is, the cycle of life, dude. We can't have three generations co-existing here in Robat; that'd be crazy!" explained Turk.

"Would it though? I don't see the problem," said Tom.

"Oh, really? So, there would be like three generations; a first, second and third? That means they would be like double parents and half kids or something?" said Turk like it was the most absurd thing he had ever heard.

"No, I think the first generation would be like big parents and the third generation like small kids," Indarra suggested. "Anyway, that's just how it is: there were always only two generations. Otherwise, you would need a dif-ferent form of organization. Besides, there wouldn't be enough room for everyone."

"Yeah, you're right, that does sound better."

"Thank you, Tom."

"Well, I think all of this sounds super cool!" exclaimed Ross.

"It still makes no sense. Why would you go and march up there to your death so willingly? Look, guys, if we have kids, and they become our age, would you do it just because it looks like our parents did? No way! I think they must have gone there for food, but something went wrong. We know there was something going on with the food, so I think they went up there to retrieve a seed or something," said Indarra.

"Right, crops grow at different depths, and sometimes soil needs to rest for a few years because it becomes infertile or something unless you use different crops and their roots go to a different depth then you're good to go," explained Tom feeling important.

Indarra looked at him impressed and half opened her mouth a couple times thinking she could place a bit of her own knowledge too, for the good of the community, of course.

"So, you think they all went in the middle of the night to get a seed for growing diversity?" asked Ross looking doubtful.

"Right and they didn't tell us because they didn't want us to worry," added Turk somehow not noticing that his brother was being skeptical.

"But something went horribly wrong!" finished Indarra having absolutely picked up on the fact that it was improbable.

Turk clapped his hands and faked tearing up a little. "So dramatic, I just love it!"

"If only there was a job that would include entertaining people by reproducing live moments of life with an audience, we would be perfect for the job!" said Ross looking at his brother.

"Speaking of which, girls, we men have a job to do so grab your dried fruit and peanut bags!" said Ross.

Once Turk and Ross had finished giving out breakfasts for the morning and clearing out the room, the four of them headed down to the beach to the twins' house. Their house was incredible with three bedrooms, three and a half bathrooms, and a living room the size of a tennis court. It was at least twice the size of Tom and Indarra's houses although the décor was very similar to the same warm underground military base chic decor! Beds were all oversized mattresses on low stepped podiums and nightstands were units built into the wall – none of the furniture was movable. Walls were made of polished concrete and the floors were an anthracite polished single slate of wood. All the bathrooms had a large walk-in shower with walls made of a darker concrete with only one knob and a single oversized rain showerhead. The toilet was black and looked like it was suspended in midair out of the wall just like the sink and the mirror that was incrusted deep in the wall. All the windows were really large and let a lot of light into the dark structure. The windows were electric; you only had to push on a button for a heavy mechanism to push itself out a little and then slide laterally out on the wall to let the light white curtains fly. The living room was bigger than Indarra's but similar. In the left corner was the U-shaped kitchen. Its cabinets were dark eggplant and the counters were a single slate of anthracite wood like the floor. Everything was thick, heavy, and meant to last so if you came back in 60 years it would still be fine as the materials were of such great quality. You could not find a wallpaper that would fall, paint that would crack, or even a skinny loose knob in the houses. In the kitchen was a massive dining table and, to the right, a sitting area designed as a large open space. Like the rest of the house, everything was massive, thick, and solidly anchored to the ground. Three large sofas were placed around a coffee table. They were made of concrete with oversized throw pillows in different shades of grey and a few ocher ones. The living room's double doors opened onto the patio, which led out to the beach. The house was incredible and yet understated, like a beautiful comfortable stylish prison. Why the kitchen? I never got an answer to that one.

"Cool place!" exclaimed Tom as he walked around the room. Surprisingly, he had never visited the twin's house. Robatians were using communal spaces to socialize while their home were private.

"Wow, it is really nice!" added Indarra. "Do you have any other sets of twins living here?"

"Is it really much bigger than your houses? Never thought about it!" said Ross modestly.

Once Indarra was done poking the pillows and Tom had walked around the room long enough for it to get boring, they all headed upstairs.

Turk went ahead and opened a door. "Tom, you can have our parents' room at the back and Indarra, you'll sleep in my room, and I'll move in with Ross. Just let me move my things."

Tom walked over and put his hands on his hips looking at the twins suspiciously. "How is this so easy?"

Ross answered for his brother. "Everything in our relationship is based on bets. As Indarra starved herself over the baby carrots and sardines the other day, I don't have to move!" When Indarra rolled her eyes, Ross added, "Consider yourself a lucky girl, I'm disgusting."

"Great, I'm so thankful!" she said while marching into her own new room.

They all said good night and went to bed. It was weird for Indarra to be in a different room to the one she had slept in her whole life, although they were very similar. She thought of her parents that night who she probably would never see again and then started thinking of Tom's mom who she loved very much. She wondered why such great and smart people would walk to their death like this for no reason and couldn't bring herself to be at peace with the fact she'd never see them here again; the thought was terrifying! She knew she had heard something on that mountain and was convinced it was her parents and they had gone there to save them, to save her but it had gone wrong. She suddenly was convinced they were not dead but in danger and the more they waited the smaller the chance of seeing them again. She decided in the morning she would go up that mountain and save them. The thought should have been terrifying but it was exhilarating. She tried to fall asleep but could hear snoring from all over the house; her mom snored too, but not this bad . . .

She knew the boys would either wanna tag along with her or try and stop her and neither of those was an option. After hours of thinking and moving around her bed and pacing the room, she finally fell asleep to wake up a couple hours later to noises coming from the living room. The boys were up, had gone to the forum, and cooked. She was so impressed, everything looked incredible, so much that she ignored the cherry tomatoes and just smiled for they had given so much of themselves to make this place homely and to improve whatever dysfunctional family they would ultimately become.

Ross was spreading tapenade on toast when he saw Indarra. "Well, morning there! Are you in for a little Lunfast?"

"Is it really 10:30 AM?" asked Indarra a bit confused.

"Yep, we all needed the sleep," said Tom who was going through a pile of books.

"You guys are incredible, thank you so much." Indarra walked around the table smelling each dish and smiled. She thought if this was her last meal, it was going to be an awesome one.

"So what now?" asked Turk with a mouthful of devil eggs.

"I guess we keep on living," said Tom. "It feels purposeless doesn't it?"

"I don't know. We've got a whole bunch of new things going on that are pretty amazing so it doesn't seem purposeless to me!" exclaimed Ross.

Indarra looked at her friends and played nervously with her devil egg without actually eating it. "Guys, after breakfast—"

"Lunfast!" interrupted Turk.

52

"Right, Lunfast, sorry, well, after that, I'm heading to the mountain, alone. I think our parents are still there and I wanna save them. Before you start being brave, I will tell you why it would be cowardly and selfish to come with me! If you guys die, the others will starve as no one can cook or has time for it since they all have their hands full. And you, Tom . . ." she pointed at him as she could see he was going to protest, and her voice was shaking, " . . . are the teacher's son. Everyone keeps you busy all day asking you things about their own jobs and only you can answer those questions. If one of you guys took a day off, the whole community would collapse. What I need you to do is keep doing your jobs. Do not tell anyone I went up there and please tell me everything you know about that mountain."

"It kills people, Indarra, that's what we know," said Ross feeling powerless.

"My mom always told me I could move mountains," said Tom, without much of a reason.

Indarra looked at Tom for a moment.

Turk hadn't noticed what was going on and added, "I heard there are creatures in that mountain that can swallow you up if you get too close to them."

"Like from your feet up or from your upper body down if you get too close to the steep wall up there where they live," added his brother as if they had rehearsed it before.

"Well, that's stupid; if it wanted to swallow you it wouldn't wait for you to brush shoulders with it, it would just swallow you from your feet up!" said Tom forgetting all about what they had just talked about.

Turk thought about it for a moment and then agreed. "You're probably right. Well, maybe it's just from your feet up then."

"Guys, I don't think we believe the mountain really is alive and that it can swallow you. It is dangerous but if I take the right precautions and I'm quiet I think I can make it," said Indarra.

"You crazy girl!" said Turk while tapping her on the forehead.

"Alright, let's gather everything I need! Can you get me one of those bags you carry food in and make something that I can wrap around me so my hands are free? Also, I'll need water, food, and maybe like a long stick to protect myself."

"Done! Anything else?" asked Ross.

"Yes, do it fast and don't walk me to the fields. It will look too suspicious."

By the time Indarra had showered, the boys were back with Robat's first ever backpack. Indarra walked up to them with a towel wrapped around her hair and grabbed the bag. "Good job, alright, see you tonight; make me something good, I'll be exhausted."

Turk grabbed Indarra's hands and silently looked into her eyes for a while. When he opened his mouth she expected one of his rare moments of seriousness. Instead, he said, "Indarra, if monsters eat you, remember you're worth it as you'll feed many of them!"

They all laughed, hugged, and Indarra headed out of the house. She didn't know what to expect, how long it would take her to make it to her parents or wherever she was going, or if she'd get back alive. She turned right, walked by the beach, and then turned right again to walk by the edge of the village; she didn't want to be seen on the main street fleeing with that bag. A couple minutes later, she made it to the fields and could see the silo to her right. A few people, including Deborah, were working in the fields but they were far too busy to notice her so she casually walked through the field and made it to where the land began to rise.

From up close it looked like irregular steps with a bit of vegetation covering it but not as dense a layer as it looked from the village. She carefully tempted a first step expecting the land to swallow her, but nothing happened. Then, both her feet were on the mountain but still nothing. Her first few steps were hesitant and she was very careful. Everything was new and maneuvering around the vegetation wasn't exactly easy, but soon she gained confidence. Walking uphill wasn't something she was used to and even though she was athletic, she quickly got really tired. When her thighs felt like they were on fire she decided to sit for a bit. As she turned around for the first time to sit and face the valley an incredible feeling of dizziness suddenly took over her body. An invisible force seemed to draw her from the ground below. She wondered if that's what they had meant about being swallowed by the mountain as this was the feeling she had. She lay back, closed her eyes, and started breathing deep and slowly. Her cold sweat stopped and it slowly started drying off her body as a calm feeling came over her. After a while, she finally reopened her eyes and tried to sit up, but not all the way. She rested her weight on her elbows and tried to look at the village. She could do it in this position and it was the most incredible thing she'd ever seen. Watching something from above was just incredible. She quickly sat up and just stared with her mouth open. She could see everything; she had never seen her village as a whole or the roof of her house before. Everything and everyone looked so small. She could see the ocean as if it would never end, and the coral reef and the waves breaking on it. The immensity of the ocean made the lagoon seem so tiny. She could see the beach, just a thin strip of yellow, the roofs of the buildings, and people walking about though she couldn't tell who they were. In the fields right below her, she thought she might have recognized Deborah. Then, she noticed that the star was no longer shining on the horizon but from the middle of the sea. Indarra thought it was weird but after all that had happened in such a short amount of time, this was just another small event.

She hadn't walked for long enough to think about eating so she only had a sip of water and got back to her feet while turning back towards the mountain – she didn't feel like facing the valley while standing just yet. She was happy to be alive and to witness such incredible things but didn't know where to search for her parents and the rest of the First Generation. It was frankly disappointing not to have found anything yet, but she thought that the further up she went the more she'd be able to see and once she was on top, she'd have a view of the whole bay, which also meant she'd see them if they were on the mountain. The mountain seemed to wrap itself around the village and its arms seemed to plunge in the water around it in a way that seemed to make it joined to the coral reef. It was easy to get a clear view of the whole mountain. She had kept on the left side of the mountain since it was the straightest route from where she had started. She walked for a bit longer and suddenly felt like the hike was getting much easier as she neared the top. When the ground was almost flat under her feet, she decided it would be safe to turn around while standing. She made a slow rotation on her left foot and almost fell backward as the view she'd had earlier of the village was nothing compared to what she saw now! The ocean now seemed to extend a thousand times further than the distance between the beach and the reef. The water was colors of shades she'd never seen before. She could see dark blues, lighter ones, and also some green patches. The fields seemed to be moving like water under the wind. She stayed there for a moment staring at the splendid vista and then remembered why she was there, so she started scanning the mountain for traces of the First Generation. Surely, dozens of people on that mountain should be easy to spot, but she searched and searched again but she couldn't see anything. The mountain was just the same stony matter with this thin green layer of grass on it, nothing more. It seemed like this was all for nothing. She was safe, but her parents clearly hadn't walked up the mountain or they would have turned back down and been fine. Plus, there was clearly no vegetables worth getting from the mountain to plant back down in Robat. As she looked around she thought she saw a dark shadow move further down but decided not to scare herself unless danger was imminent.

She still wasn't hungry and decided to save her food for the way down. It hadn't taken long to get up there so she didn't think she'd actually be hungry and need her bag, which was slowing her down, but decided she wouldn't leave it there as she didn't want to waste the food. Instead, she decided to take a long break to admire the view as she didn't know when she would return there again. She was happy to be alone in a place like this and to see such beautiful scenery. She also wondered if she should maybe lie to her friends of the many dangers she had encountered so that no one would dare going up there and spoil her haven!

She changed her mind slightly about the place when she heard a crack. Her whole body tensed up and she pulled the branch out of her backpack ready to protect herself from what would probably cause her death. She was scared like she had never been and further from home than ever. Whatever it was, was getting closer. Footsteps approached her, much heavier than her own, and she was sure the creature coming towards her must be enormous. There was no way she could protect herself with that stupid stick. Then she saw him coming from out of the shadowy part of the mountain. It turns out the big creature was Tom.

"Well, hey there! How funny; us bumping into each other like this. What's up? Do you come here often?" he added in a flirty manner.

"Tom! What are you doing here? You weren't supposed to come! You scared me to death!"

"Well, I'm selfish, and I was worried for you, so I'm here. I was never going to let you go up here on your own, so I followed you and hid when you turned around."

"Well, that's really nice but crazy. Did you find out anything?"

"Yeah, do you sleep on your back? Your hair is all flat behind your head."

"Oh, shut up! Well, I didn't find anything either. This is so weird; if I didn't see you this whole time, could it be that they are on the mountain but we can't see them? Although, I think I did see you when I was sitting on the mountain earlier."

"Yeah, I was trying not to move but a spider climbed onto my leg. However, I think we would have seen them because I was just one person and I was hiding. They are a large group and I don't think they would be trying to hide. If they were on the mountain, we would have seen them. Damn it, I was so sure and excited about it. This seemed like such a risky thing to do that I knew we'd see them. Know what I mean?"

"Yeah, I know. Is it weird I'm kind of happy? The take-over and all, this is just so exciting!"

"I guess, it could be worse, but it's just strange. Why do it this way? Why now? Why couldn't they wait a little longer to plan the transition and train us? Why do it over-night like this?" said Tom, not sounding upset, just questioning his new reality.

"I know, maybe that's just how it always is and somehow, with time, we'll find out that this is how it has always been and we'll follow the same path and leave our own children in a state of incomprehension. To be fair, I don't think I wanna have my own Second Generation to take care of."

"That's ridiculous, Indarra, what would you do?"

"Excuse me!" said Indarra offended.

"That's not what I meant, I just wanna say that this is what we do! That's our main goal," stated Tom.

"Is it though? Can't I decide what my main goal is? Honestly, I love you, I love that I get to love people, I love that I get to not like you if I want to, I love that I don't have to fake loving you, it would suck if I suddenly stopped, but that's what makes our relationship so awesome and real. We both know how we feel about it; you're an amazing friend and that's just how it is. Are you allowed not to love your kids? I don't think you can. And even if I did love my kid, I would always wonder if maybe I just thought I loved them because I had to, or maybe I truly loved them and somehow would stop loving them at some point. That would be awful because I couldn't just be like, 'Sorry, I'm done, your company no longer entertains me.' Seriously,

Tom, I just don't think that it's my thing." She dropped the twig she had been savaging for the past 10 minutes and started to get up. "Shall we?"

"You're kidding, right?"

"What?"

"Aren't you curious to know what's on the other side?"

"There's no other side, it just ends."

"So, you think there's a wall? And then what's behind it?"

"Right, I get your point. Do you think it could be dangerous though? Can we just go? You know?"

"Well, we were freaked out at the idea of even approaching that mountain. Just a bit earlier, you cautiously tapped the rock with your foot as if it were made of shark teeth, just like an idiot, and now we're standing at the top of it. I think it's safe to say we've been lied to and nothing's gonna happen if we take a few more steps."

"Why would they lie to us about it though? I don't know," whispered Indarra thinking aloud. "So, shall we?"

They marched to the very top of the mountain with no idea of what to expect. Would there be a wall? More mountain going further into the sky? Emptiness? Thoughts coursed through their minds but the main question was, 'why haven't they thought about it before?' Why hadn't their minds gone passed that mountain? And then they saw it!

"What the . . . ?" exclaimed Indarra.

"Oh, crap! Is that our village?"

Chapter 4

THE RULER

"Well, that makes no sense, how can we be on both sides?"

"Well, I guess that explains the whole question of 'how can a mountain have walls?' We've simply gone around."

"Around? Around what? Look behind you, genius, you can see our village on both sides.

"Err, right. I guess around is not the right word, but the idea is there as it's better than a wall. It obviously loops back in some flat way, unless you can think of another word that describes a flat loop?"

"So, do you think that if we go back this way, we'll end up back to our village as if I had gone right when I left Robat earlier?"

"Well, yeah I think, so let's try the new path."

They started walking downhill on the new path towards the right side of the village. It appeared to be a lot harder than going uphill. They were still scanning the mountain, hoping to find the First Generation or hoping not to?

"Does it feel different?" asked Tom while cautiously walking over a bush.

"What does?"

"This, the mountain."

"Hmmm, I don't know, not really, does it for you?"

"Does it what?"

"Feel different you idiot!"

"Oh, right, not really, I guess not, I don't know, maybe?

"Well, it is different. We went up on the left side and now we're coming down from the right side which means we'll arrive by the barn and then my old house, so it is different."

"Oh, that's interesting, true! We are going on the right side, I guess it makes sense if it makes us loop flat," said Tom satisfied with his new phrase.

"Aha, loop flat, I love it." Indarra stopped walking. "The school is bigger."

"It does look bigger."

"It does not 'look' bigger, it is bigger! There's an extra room at least! Look! Ours is a simple square whereas this one is like a big L-shaped-building."

"Oh, wow, we haven't only looped flat, we also went into the future!"

"Or had a super long nap without noticing it," joked Indarra.

They walked down for a while to what they thought was Robat, until it became obvious this was a different place, everyone was dressed differently and looked different, even from afar. In fact, they had not recognized a single Robatians. Even though the place was basically the same, it had a cleaner, more utilitarian look. Tom and Indarra should have picked up on this before they saw the shape of the school. Robat's buildings were white while this village was bare concrete. It was amazing that by walking down the other side of a mountain, their first thought when they saw a new village appear was time travel.

"I don't think the twins would have started scratching all the paint out of our buildings facades out of sadness though. Tom, this is not our village."

"How is that possible? How are we living a couple hours walk away from another village and none of us know about it?"

"I guess if everyone has been freaked about the mountain, then it would not be hard for two villages to be two hours away without knowing about one another. Of course, both villages would need to feel the same way about that mountain."

"After all we've been through, I'm like a blank page. I can basically take in all the weird stuff you'll throw at me, but that one really is crazy."

They stood there for a while wondering what they should do next. They couldn't stay there forever and they sure couldn't go back to their village and forget about this crucial piece of information. At first, Tom wanted to go straight to the village and just tell everyone that they were from a place called Robat on the other side of the mountain. Indarra wanted to go back to Robat and tell people about it to set up a plan about how to introduce both civilizations. Or maybe they should just tell the twins first? They ended up compromising, that is, picking Indarra's second idea.

"What if we just hide for a while in the village and, you know, try to find out more information about these people. Who are they? Are they dangerous? Maybe they're the keepers of the mountain and know about us already!" said Indarra.

"Why? What would be the purpose of being the keeper of a dead rock?"

"I don't know, maybe there's something there we could have found but didn't because it's too big. Perhaps they were supposed to keep us from crossing it but they were too busy trying to kill fish with a ruler!"

"Aha, so funny! That one actually is hitting the water with a ruler!" said Tom, looking at a man trying to kill a fish by hitting the surface of the water repeatedly with a ruler.

"Right, seeing this, I don't think we're in immediate danger, but it is still better to keep a low profile and spy for a while. It looks very much like our village so it should be easy to get around."

After making it to the flat grounds of the village, they hid behind the barn as there was no one working there. They looked to their right and couldn't see anyone on the other side in the fields. They figured everyone must be closer to the beach. They slowly ventured towards the path, which, in Robat, would have gone down to the beach, or if you turned right, to Indarra's house. It was even scarier than getting on the mountain back in Robat, because if they were caught they had no idea what could happen. However, they couldn't go back now as their curiosity was too strong and too much was happening. They wanted to get to know the people and find out if co-operation was an option. They walked closer and heard a voice.

"You're doing it all wrong, Paul, just give it to me! See, if you hit it with the flat of the ruler, then the strength of your blow will be equally distributed over the total area of its skull, that is to say about four square centimeters, whereas, if you hit it with the corner, like this, you'll break right through it! Well, it didn't work this time because the ruler is probably not pointy enough, but that's the general idea."

"What the?" started Indarra.

"Let's run for our life!" laughed Tom.

"I hope I never have to meet that one."

"Could you see where the voice was coming from?"

"Well, I'm guessing they were either in the sea or by a house trying to murder a fish and failing."

Then they heard another girl speak. "Where is Victor? We're clearly bad at it. His mother used to fish so he must know how to do it."

"I'll go look for him," said the crazy ruler girl.

The steps approached in their direction so they ran to the back of the village and hid in the barn. It was like theirs with a semi-open area so that animals could shelter from the rain but could also be in the sun if they wanted to. It was never cold so a proper building was not necessary. It was cozy, but a bit overcrowded, at least, this one was. The one in Robat was not as packed. They must eat less meat here thought Indarra. They sat on the ground in the straw, their backs against the wall. This way they could see if someone came along on, planning to hide in the straw if they did.

"That girl was a total nightmare," said Tom.

"I guess she was hmmm, rather unbearable," tried Indarra.

"She made me miss Deborah!"

"Right, enough gossiping about the faceless girl."

"Do we even know if they're human?"

"Tom, you saw them from the mountain 30 minutes ago."

"Right, sorry."

"Well, we've learned something crucial already! They're going through the same phase."

"You mean the transition?"

"Well, of course, that bossy girl, whatever her name is," she said while playing with the straw, she had found more twigs to traumatize. "was clearly struggling with that fish because the First Generation wasn't around anymore to do it for them. And that Victor guy's mother must have been a fisher back then."

"That would explain the screams or the mutter you heard; that wasn't our parents from the mountain, it was them!"

"Right, they must have woken up a little bit earlier than us and what I heard was them finding out about the transition right before we did."

"It could be, what should we do next?"

"We should go hide in the bushes by the beach, wait for the end of dinner, then, when they walk back, we go and sleep in one of the unoccupied houses. If they did what we did, some of them must have decided to share houses so as not to be alone at night. We can also have dinner in the bushes since we have my bag of food."

They walked out of the barn and back to the path to the beach; they didn't meet anyone as the locals must have been working on dinner or maybe even be eating by then. They could now see the beach. It was just like theirs with the same houses with their patios and lounge chairs outside. There were only a few noticeable differences such as the color of the walls and an almost clinical look about everything. The patios in Robat looked inviting and comfy while those looked like somewhere you'd have a business meeting. They could now see the school from up close and it was so big it used up part of the beach and blocked the view on the other side of the village where the twins house would have been. They sat there quietly, eating what was supposed to be Indarra's food for her wild adventure. Beef sausages, rosemary roasted potatoes, and pumpkin pies were on the menu, the twins had been kind! Tom was the most scared of them both, however, as he had always been sort of left out this was the most exciting thing he had ever done, and doing it with Indarra was awesome. He loved her so very much, like a sister. She, on the other hand, was more nervous about the responsibility she had there. She knew if something happened, she would be the one in charge. Tom was smart and brave in his own way, but she was tougher and had more experience in all sorts of things. Tom's dad had died when he was very little. Maggie raised him by herself, well, with the community, but still, she did an excellent job. It was a difficult job on Robat to be a parent and a teacher as you had to teach your own child. When your mother is gutting chickens out back, she is just a mother once she returns home at night. But when you're a teacher, you're your child's teacher 24/7. She tried not to, but it was difficult to separate both things, besides, to be fair, it had made Tom very knowledgeable about so many things. Tom and Indarra rarely spoke about Tom's father. Pre-transition death was something uncommon in Robat, so no one really knew how to deal with it and how to talk about it. Maggie never seemed very sad but more hurt by the sadness it had caused her child. Tom had been affected by the event. He had been mocked by the other kids and a lot of people put the fact that he was slightly different from the other kids down to his father's death. Indarra didn't think any of it had to be explained, but she didn't think the lack of a father had made him different, but the way people treated him for lacking one did.

A long while after they finished their meal, they started hearing the locals walking towards the beach. They heard them speak and some seemed happy sounding. Things seemed to be working fine there. They couldn't see what was happening on the other side of the beach behind the school since the school blocked the view in this village, but they could see the houses filling up with groups of people on this side of the beach. It was hard to make out faces, as they were too far away but they had seemed human from the mountain. Their voices sounded slightly different but they were human. Tom had already pictured them with odd numbers of limbs or with corn-on-the-cob like skin. When two girls and a guy finally made it to the house at the edge of the village closest to them, they finally saw them, they were literally 10 meters away. Tom and Indarra both held their breath, convinced that if the group were to stop talking they would hear them breathe. However, when Tom shifted his weight slightly the leaves crackled under him and the closest girl turned and looked straight at them. Both their bodies tensed like ice and they couldn't breathe anymore. Thankfully, they were hidden in total darkness and in rather thick foliage. The girl obviously didn't seem to think much of it as they all entered the house.

Tom and Indarra didn't want to go into a house right away as they didn't know if another group would show up. So far, there were three empty houses left: the one at the end of the village, the one next to the one they'd seen the group enter, and the one after it. After no one showed up for another 30 minutes, the whole village seemed to be asleep and they decided to slowly venture out of the bushes and walk to the closest empty house, which would have been Indarra's in Robat. It was such a weird feeling as both houses were different, but not enough that it still felt like her house. They walked onto the patio and she put her hand on the knob, scared to find someone inside. She twisted it and the door opened without a noise.

They walked into the open plan living area of the house. It was basically like her home. The big difference was that in Robat houses were white outside but with a darker concrete finish on the inside, while this house was white from floor to ceiling. Everything was white including the furniture and appliances. It looked very medical. The only color you could find was anthracite on the kitchen countertops. Otherwise, the furniture was the same and placed in the exact same spot. They slowly walked upstairs, trying not to make a noise, which was easy on the white marble floors. They walked around the rooms, which were clearly empty, said good night, and went to bed without any plans for the day after. The adventures had been enough and they could come up with a plan in the morning. Tom was exhausted, whereas Indarra could easily handle the physical activity they'd had. For Tom it had been a challenging day, and, when combined with the mental exhaustion caused by all the changes they'd experienced, he slept like a baby. He didn't worry about what was going to happen in the morning, didn't think about the early transition, wasn't concerned about their world that had doubled in the course of a day, or think about his brother who had died the same day as his dad. His brother had occupied most of his dreams since it had happened. Tom had never forgotten that day when after school, Maggie told him that his dad and brother would not return home because they had transitioned early. No one bothered with explanations, almost as if it didn't matter, and he never asked how they died. Tom often wondered if one day he'd wake up and find out that Indarra had died. The random way it had happened for his family made him think that it could happen any time without him expecting it at all. These fears fed many of his dreams, but not tonight and Tom had a wonderful dreamless sleep. Nothing could have woken him up, expect a blow on the head obviously.

"If you attack me, I will scream and all my friends in the house next door will hear me. The wind is now blowing towards the right side of the beach and will carry my voice with ease."

Tom recognized the voice right away, it was the ruler-know-it-all he had heard the day before. She was standing right by the bed with a defiant look on her face.

"Oh, hello," said Tom casually. "Is this your room?"

"I'm sorry, does this seem like the appropriate answer to my last statement?"

"Please don't scream. Nobody knows we're here."

"We?" she said terrified and started screaming, "help!"

"No, please, please stop," he backed as far as he could from her in the bed, holding his hand in front of him to show he didn't want to harm her.

Indarra rushed into the room at the commotion.

"We're so sorry but please be quiet and listen to us for a minute," said Indarra. "I will move away from the doorway so that after we're done talking you can scream and run for your safety if you want. but please listen first." Indarra slowly shifted to her right and away from the door.

"Who are you and what are you doing in my house?" the girl asked.

"Well, I believe you and I have both spent the past 20 something years in the same house."

"That's crazy!"

"I come from a village just like yours and we were raised to believe that there was nothing but our village here. The coral reef kept the sharks on one side and the mountain at the back of the village provided a convenient prison for us. I believe the same happened to you. Someone wanted to keep us apart. Two days ago, all our parents disappeared. Yesterday, we went up the mountain because we thought we heard them there, but now I know that what we heard yesterday was you guys, witnessing your parents' early transition a few minutes before we did in Robat."

"Robat?"

"That's our village," said Tom reminding everyone he was in the room too.

"Our village is called Robin," declared the girl.

"That's an odd name," said Indarra looking at Tom who was making a face at the sound of the word.

"There's nothing odd about it, it's our village," said the girl, sounding offended.

Indarra put her hand to her mouth when she realized she had been insensitive. "I'm sorry, this is all so new."

"And how did you go from your village to ours?"

"Well, we walked up that mountain in search for our parents and we made it to the top. We saw your village on the other side and at first, we thought it was ours again, but then we walked down and started noticing differences," explained Tom

"You can't reach the mountain – it's impossible, there's a force field around it. We have its equation and have been working for generations on a way to neutralize it. You are liars, I will scream for help."

Indarra rushed towards her and pleaded from a shorter distance so the girl could see the truthful expression in her eyes. It took the girl by surprise and somehow she did not scream. "I promise you, we've been told lies our whole life. I only walked on that mountain out of desperation thinking I'd die doing it. Where I'm from we've been told that there were creatures guarding the mountain and that the mountain itself could eat you up. I mean come on!" Indarra almost sounded exasperated now. "We're right here in front of you, we couldn't have hidden all this time in the village; we have to be from some other place."

"Well, that's what bothers me," said the girl more calmly this time. "Yesterday, all our parents disappeared and today you guys somehow found a way to a new village across the mountain."

"Not suddenly, we heard you guys," said Tom moving slightly out of the blanket and almost lifting a hand to get permission to speak.

"How can I trust you? You haven't brought up any real proof of what you're saying. Am I supposed to believe what you say and introduce you to my peers? And then what? You make us all disappear in the middle of the night like you did our parents?"

"Wait, what? That makes no sense. If we wanted to do that, why would we stay this exposed in one of your houses." Indarra could feel the blood rushing to her face.

"Good point, why would you? Unless you wanted me to find you so that I could tell everyone your story. You hope that people will be hopeless enough to believe your little tale and then you can take over."

"Take what over?" Indarra was almost screaming now and Tom gestured at her to be quieter, so she continued, her voice so low that the girl actually stepped closer to her. "Please, think about it. What do you think we could possibly want? What is the worst scenario you can think of?"

"I don't know," she said lost and confused. "I can't think right now."

Tom got up from the bed this time. "There's nothing, we're just people like you. We're confused and scared and my head hurts from whatever you hit me with."

"It was a ruler . . ."

"With the corner? Damn, I'm gonna smell like fish," said Tom scratching his head.

"What?"

"We got here yesterday in the afternoon. When we arrived we found shelter behind the last house and we heard you. Then we hid in the bushes during dinner to wait for a free house," explained Indarra.

"How did you know there would be one?"

"Because we did exactly what you did and moved in together. I was living in this exact house back in Robat but Tom and I left our respective houses last night to move in with the twins."

"Twins? Is that a name?"

"No, it's Turk and Ross."

"Why do you call them that then?"

"Because they're twins," said Tom confused.

"What is that?"

"It's two siblings born the same day who look exactly alike."

"It simply can't be; this doesn't exist."

"Could we please focus? Anyway, we figured friends would gather together as we did. We all missed our parents, we were scared. We are scared," she continued trying to establish common ground with the girl. "Please, we're desperate, we need your help to figure out what's going on. We wanna find our parents and we wanna go home."

"Adimen," said the girl calmly this time.

"What?" asked Tom.

"That's my name, I'm Adimen."

"I'm Indarra and that's my best friend, Tom. And our friends Turk and Ross, the ones we now live with, they know we left. Well, they know I left . . . Tom, do they know where you are?"

Their greetings were kind of awkward as no one ever had to do it before.

"No, I didn't tell anyone."

"They'll probably think we died, I don't think they'll come to look for us."

Chapter 5

THE GEOLOGIST

It was sunny in Robin, really sunny and warm, the type of warm where the sun feels great on your skin without making you sweat too much and where the shade has this gentle refreshing breeze but is still warm enough that you can be in your bathing suit without feeling a chill every time the breeze intensifies. What else could one want? Perhaps a colorful reef full of fish, an ocean clearer than glass that displayed every shade of green and blue imaginable, a beach with the thinnest white sand, and an incredibly beautiful mountain towering over this little paradise. Robin truly was a wonderful place and it would be difficult to feel unhappy in such a place, but of course, humans are humans, and on this day, in particular, Robinians were not having a great time.

"Who would want to be your friend you freak! How about you go play with your friends, the rocks!" said the boy.

Everyone around Adimen started laughing. Her face went red and her eyes filled with tears as she ran from the beach and went to the only place she knew she'd be safe.

W ell, we need to have a good long conversation," Adimen said and walked to the back of the bedroom where Tom had spent the night. She pushed a button to close the blinds all the way. "I'm gonna make coffee. You guys wait here, you can't venture near the windows. I'll go downstairs to shut all the electric blinds."

Only Adimen didn't make coffee for her new guests but pushed the hallway cabinet in front of the bedroom door trapping Indarra and Tom inside. "I'm sorry guys," she called. "You have a bathroom in there and you have water, but I can't let you out right now. Please don't scream, I will be back."

"What? What are you doing? You can't leave us here like this; people will be looking for us!" Indarra said desperately.

"No, they won't, you said as much. Just relax; I'll be back in the morning," said Adimen.

"No, no! Wait!" Tom banged on the door, but Adimen had already left.

"What do you think she is gonna do?" said Tom while putting all his weight on the door.

"I don't know. I don't think she means us harm. She is just trying to protect herself. What would we have done if we had found someone we didn't know in our house?"

"I don't like her! She's weird, bossy, annoying, and her eyes are stupid."

"Don't be mean; they're beautiful, they're so light, and they're clear like water."

"I don't care for it, it makes her look inhuman."

"Tom, you stop this right away! Good night!"

They both went to bed quietly. They had never shared a bed with anyone before and while it didn't feel that weird to them, it was just weird that at this moment when they were physically so close, it was also the only time there had ever been tension between them. Indarra had never snapped at him like that before; in fact, the only time Tom had seen her upset was at other people when she was protecting him. Prisoners or not, it was the middle of the night and there was nothing better to do than sleep. A few hours later, Indarra woke up to a noise coming from downstairs. She got out of bed and noticed that the door was now slightly open. She slowly walked out of the room into the hallway and down the stairs. Adimen was reheating food in the kitchen and had placed three plates on the dining table.

"I thought you guys would be hungry. Did you pack enough food for the whole trip yesterday?" asked Adimen casually as if she hadn't locked up her guests for hours. "I hope you like poached eggs. I'm not that great a cook but if you boil them the right amount of time there's no reason why they shouldn't be poached! Should you go wake up Tom? He's probably hungry too and I don't want all this food to get cold."

"Sure, thank you," said Indarra, unsure if she should be thankful or run for her life seeing this lunatic now acting so normal. She could have chosen the latter but decided otherwise. "You're not about to lock us again are you?"

"Well, don't be silly! Why would I free you to lock you up again? It wouldn't make any sense!"

"Right, I'll go get Tom then."

Indarra started walking back upstairs but looked back at Adimen a couple times, trying to comprehend the bizarre conversation they'd just had. They all sat around the table and started eating their breakfast; the eggs were overcooked and the potatoes were tasteless but they were starving and it was food!

"Why did you free us?" asked Indarra in between two mouthfuls of disappointing eggs.

"I had to check if an old memory was real or not." She turned and looked at Tom. "Excuse me, do you have to eat like an animal?"

Indarra glanced over at Tom who was devouring his potatoes with no grace. She rolled her eyes in an amused yet patronizing way and then looked at Adimen with hate. "Why did you return home in the middle of the night?" asked Indarra dismissing the comment about Tom.

"Because it's my house and I live here."

"But why in the middle of the night? Everyone else had gone home hours ago."

"I don't believe I need to justify when I enter or leave my own house now do I?"

"No, of course not, sorry."

Tom muttered under his breath, "It does look suspicious though."

"I was working on the problem we're all facing if you must know! That's what people do when they face a situation like this, which is also what you should have done before wandering on the mountain with no preparation. You could have died!" She sounded like a worried parent about to punish her kids so they never put themselves in danger again. It was almost cute, above all because it came from Adimen! Pulling herself together she added. "What's your village like?"

"From what we've seen, they're nearly identical," said Indarra.

"Nearly? Do you have the sharks behind the coral reef?" Tom nodded

"Twelve houses, a forum, a school, a roundhouse, a barn, and a silo?

"Yes, there are differences but they are subtle. Your school is bigger and our houses are white on the outside but darker on the inside," said Indarra trying to get a piece of eggshell out of her eggs.

"Your barn contains more animals than ours," said Tom, although it almost sounded like a question.

"Our village looks more laid back I would say," added Indarra.

"You look so athletic," said Adimen suddenly grabbing Indarra's muscular arms.

"Really?" Indarra was blushing. "Not really. Why is your school bigger? Are there more Second Generation here than in our village?"

"Sixteen here in Robin."

"About the same, so why is it bigger? How many hours do you spend there every day?"

"About 10 hours a day."

"What? That's insane! How can you stand being locked up in that building for 10 hours?" said Tom, potatoes falling out of his mouth.

"It's fascinating what we do at school, really! We learn so much and what else would we spend our time doing anyway?"

"I don't know, spend time outside, and swim!"

"We do practice sports an hour every four days, to keep healthy . . ."

"We have school three hours per day and then we do outdoor activities for another five hours. That would explain the size of the school," said Indarra.

"Why? Why the similarities? Why the differences? How can there be two of our villages? Why didn't we know about it?" asked Adimen.

"I really don't know; maybe our civilizations got separated somehow and what one needed the other needed too, hence the extreme similarities. We need to teach the upcoming generation so there's a school like we need food so we have fields and a barn, and a forum for a gathering place. Maybe we have evolved separately but are similar because that's the only way possible. Doing it differently would have been inefficient. Moreover, the subtle differences in our villages represent the subtle differences we have as humans."

Tom gave Indarra a you-sound-cheesy look girl! He said, "I guess, well, I don't know if humans necessarily need the parental bathroom to have the shower on the left and the sink on the right side and the opposite for the Second Generation. Kinda seems like a random thing and not a necessity."

"True, it could also be a coincidence, or perhaps building a square-shaped house is logical. Plus, right-handed people usually start working from the left whatever they do so the parental suite, which is the one they start with, will always be on the left!" Indarra looked at Tom in annoyance. She could not understand why he wouldn't back her up. "It's therefore logical to place the sink on the left and the shower on the other side since the closet is in the wall there."

"A little far-fetched, but why not." That was as convinced as Tom was gonna get.

"What should we do? Should we tell people yet? I have a plan either way!" exclaimed Adimen excitedly and she went on to explain her overly thought out plans. She had a whole thing about how they could share all their information about both places to create one bigger village where the tasks would be redistributed according to the needs of a 32-person First Generation population. New kind of jobs would be created and everything optimized in a very boring way and tasks would be repetitive. Taylorism would finally make it to Robat and Robin. Tom grimaced the whole time. Adimen noticed but didn't pay any attention. There was a whole food repartition program that Indarra disapproved of as it included small living things and they realized that the nutrients offered by Adimen wouldn't be enough back in Robat.

The second plan was much simpler; Tom and Indarra would go back to Robat and none of them would ever mention the other village and go back to their normal lives. Well, as normal as it could be considering the early transition had happened barely 48 hours before. They briefly considered the second idea since they thought that telling the population about each other might be too much to handle considering the recent trauma. However, it now seemed impossible to go back and forget what they had just seen. Besides, Adimen was curious about Robat now she had heard of it and she wanted to see it for her own eyes. So they decided they would not tell anyone just yet and assess the situation a little longer until they found a better way to make it all work. After all, they were in no rush as the transition had only just happened. Tom and Indarra couldn't hide forever in Robin, but as there was only one resident in the house, they could keep living in it until they worked out a plan.

"You guys will hide out here and only come out at night when everyone is asleep if really necessary. I'll bring food here and no one else will enter this house. I think the best thing to do, for now, is to see how things go in Robin and we will formulate a plan accordingly.

"Waiting, that's your solution? What do we have to wait for?" asked Tom.

"Adimen is right, Tom, nothing bad is gonna happen in the next few days. We can see how the Robinians acclimatize to all this and then see what we do."

"Why don't we just go home and see how our people acclimatize?"

"You guys are not prisoners and you sure are free to go back, but if you do, you can't tell anyone about us, not until we've figured out something. There will be power shifting over the next few days within our villages; we already have this guy who's trying to take charge. I don't think he would be good as all he wants is power and he doesn't care about the good of the community. A lot of people will try to take on the decision making for others. Therefore, I think it's going to be difficult enough like this and if we mix our villages now, without thinking, one of them might try to take over the other one."

"What do you mean take over? Why would we take over the same village when we already have the exact same one?" asked Tom.

"I'm not necessarily talking about the land," explained Adimen. "Some people will make new friends and people will start mixing, but we have different ways of doing things so it's only natural that this will start conflict and solving conflict might imply forcing your way of doing things onto the other village. For instance, you seem to think it's OK to keep your shoes on in bed!" she said looking at Tom with furious eyes.

"I forgot to remove them. And this house is freezing!" he added seeing Indarra's accusatory look.

"Tom, I don't think there's a point in going home right now. It would take us two days to go and come back and for what? To tell the twins we're fine? That seems like a lot of energy spent over not much."

"But they think we're dead."

"That's not that terrible. Besides, soon they'll find out we're not and that will give them some fresh unpredicted happiness. Thanks to us." Indarra winked at Adimen as if they had built some kind of a bond, but Adimen did not seem to feel the same way yet.

"You sure know how to spoil your friends, don't you," joked Tom.

"You know what I mean; think about all the things we can discover here, the things we can tell Adimen, and what she can tell us about her village. We've been apart for who knows how long, maybe tens of generations, and we're finally reunited."

"I need to head out or it will look suspicious," said Adimen. "I left some things to reheat in the fridge for lunch but I will be back for dinner. I need to work."

"You have a job? What's your job?" asked Tom.

"I'm a geologist!"

"What is that? What is the job she was talking about?" Tom asked when she had gone.

"I don't know, Tom."

"I don't like her, that's what I think. Her hair looks weird and she sounds weird. I don't trust her and she's no fun!" spat Tom.

"Well, that's an understatement . . . but I think we can trust her, she seems like a decent person. Sure, we'll never be friends but nothing can keep us from being a team anyway. Tom, I think she's trustworthy."

They walked around the house and then sat on the sofa and stared into emptiness for a while. Tom got up and started snooping around, out of boredom mainly. He began in the kitchen, looking at the food. Lunch looked yummy but that's not really snooping. He compared the cutlery and then, after literally opening every drawer and cabinet on that floor, he slowly made his way up to the second floor for no particular reason. Being locked up in a house with nothing to do was enough of a reason. He walked back into the room where he had woken up and checked out her clothes and the pile of books on the desk. They were about things Tom did not really understand – the study of rocks, sedimentation layers, and notebooks with her research. Some were on the desk and others in drawers, but all of it was very tidy. One of them explained the village had more friable ground on the surface than it did deeper. Another notebook seemed to have been written when she was a child.

"Tom! Are you snooping around?" Indarra had walked upstairs and into the room without Tom noticing anything.

"No, I'm not, I was tidying up a little . . . that's it!"

"You were tidying up? You? Someone else's things? In a drawer? You were tidying up the inside of a stranger's diary?"

"Right, as you see I went the extra mile as a house guest," said Tom pretending to dust off a lamp. "Just don't mention it; I don't wanna take credit for it."

"Of course. Don't worry, I know you're such a selfless person!"

"My mom raised me well," added Tom.

"Did you find anything suspicious?" asked Indarra quietly.

"You were blaming me for snooping a minute ago!"

"I wouldn't tell you to go snoop around that girl's things but since you've already done it we might as well use the information you got from it," said Indarra while letting her fingers slide on the books and almost accidentally opening one.

"No, no, no, nothing weird, nothing worth mentioning, hmm, just things about rocks; that loser sure loves them."

"Alright then, what do you wanna do?"

"I'm a little tired so I think I'm just gonna stay here and rest for a while. It's just that . . ." Tom stopped for a moment to think. "With all that's happened lately, I think it really drained me."

"In the middle of the day? Really? Alright then. I guess it's not like there's much we can do anyway, well, good night then, or good day, I'm not sure what to call it."

"Right bye!" said Tom while gently guiding Indarra out of the room and closing the door behind her.

An hour later, Tom reappeared and sat next to Indarra who was reading in the living room. She was engrossed in a book and didn't acknowledge Tom's arrival though she obviously knew he was there. How much these people cared about studying every single detail about their village intrigued her. Nothing had been left to the unknown from the material their ground was made of to air pressure, the climate in the village, medicine, or the way butter changes its properties at different temperatures. It was exhausting. Couldn't they just leave it be? When butter was black and stank then it was burnt; there was no need to know how the water separated from the oil and lost its elasticity. Anyway, what elasticity?

"Did you know that our sharks ate 11 tons of food per year?" asked Indarra, feeling proud of her new knowledge.

"No," replied Tom, not caring much.

"Well, they eat 22 times more than the Robinians."

"Fascinating, Indarra."

"Well, these people sure think it is. Did you manage to sleep?"

"Oh, yeah, like a baby. So, Adimen isn't back," he added quickly.

"Nope."

Hours went by. Indarra kept on reading and Tom paced around the place, nervous at the idea that Adimen would be back any moment and nervous that it was not coming any sooner. Indarra seemed to find ways to keep busy and went from one book to the next, feeding Tom's obvious lack of interest with various fun facts.

She was now going through a large book about mucous. "How incredible! Human saliva has a boiling point three times that of water."

"That would make cooking pasta really hard!" laughed Tom.

"Unless you didn't need to wait for it to boil to cook the pasta in it but just needed it to reach the same temperature as water!" said Indarra.

Tom looked at Indarra. "Indarra, you're bored."

"Come on, Tom, make the best of it. You have all this free time so don't waste it sleeping. You would have done better to open a book instead," said Indarra sounding bossy. She grabbed a book from the shelf and handed it to Tom.

When Adimen returned it was 9:15 PM. She was holding a gigantic box and had to put her head to the side to see in front of her. She put it down cautiously on the kitchen counter as if it were made of glass and would shatter at the slightest vibration. "Hey, guys, sorry it's a bit late but I usually eat at work."

"Why don't you eat with everyone else?" asked Tom.

"No time. I'm always far too busy and having the same conversations over and over again at dinner is just pointless. Besides, I accomplished a lot today. I think I found something but I had to triple check my calculations. I mean, this just seemed impossible, it's just a hypothesis but the numbers simply don't lie and the probability of it being random is close to zero but how could it be?" she said really fast.

"Slow down, what do you mean? Zero probability of what?" asked Tom.

"This village could be a 120-degree sector of a circle, well, 115 . . ." declared Adimen as if she had just said the most logical thing ever.

"What? What is that?" asked Indarra looking at Tom to check if he had understood, which would have been intolerable since, after a full day of reading, she now considered herself the smart one!

"Would you say the land in Robat is exactly the same size and shape as the one here in Robin?" asked Adimen, ignoring her new companion's questions.

"Hmm, yeah, I'd say it's exactly the same, even the way the mountain curves in. If I were to stare at it from the beach, without the houses, I wouldn't be able to tell which is which. The differences are almost indiscernible," explained Indarra.

"So nothing significant if it was to be mapped?"

"I don't think so."

"How about the bay? Is it perfectly curved or does it have edges? Is it curved evenly as if you were standing on the edge of a third of a circle?"

"Oh, shit," exclaimed Indarra.

"I take this accurate scientific answer for a yes," said Adimen, while quickly scribbling something in her notebook.

"Are you saying there's a third village?" asked Tom.

"I'm not saying anything, but just look at this model." She pulled out an incredibly well detailed 3D model shaped like a croissant. "I'm just saying that if I look at a map of Robin, then add an identical village next to it – that would be Robat, right? Here on the right, there's room for another slice of the same size. Together these three slices would form a perfect circle with a huge empty mass in the middle – the mountain. Its 'arms' would extend into the valleys and in the ocean, blocking out each village on each side like a three-sided star with a circle across it, aka the coral reef."

In the model were the two villages and their houses. She had made the school smaller for Robat but got the shape slightly wrong, but it was close enough. It was the weirdest thing for Indarra and Tom to see it in model format. They now knew their village had a twin across the mountain but seeing it like this was just weird. It was so perfect in a certain way. It now seemed so accessible. The mountain, which always was an abstract frontier, now had a defined height and curves. Adimen had not made any water in the model but you could see its edges with the beach and the way the whole village curved at the back of the mountain and then the mountain itself towering over and around it and slowly plunging into the water.

"Where did you arrive in Robin?" asked Adimen while using a tape measure trying to keep it flat on the curved mountain surface.

"By the barn," said Indarra.

"So, it would be logical that you left Robat from the silo area right? Of course, that's the logical path that leads you to the barn," hurried Adimen, not really expecting an answer. She indicated their path with her finger; it looked like such a short and easy journey, much shorter than it really was. "Did you pick that trajectory on purpose?" She somehow looked at Tom.

"I don't know, I wasn't there to decide, err, it's complicated," he said and looked at Indarra.

"No, I kind of just went for it as it was quieter there," Indarra said.

"Why didn't you turn right? Then you would have ended either by our silo or the other village's silo." Adimen's tone was not accusatory.

"Hmm, I didn't think it through. I was at the twin's house that night so I went on the left path here," Indarra said and followed the path with her fingers, "so I just naturally walked to the back of the village somehow."

"Why didn't you go straight up from the beach? Why did you feel the need to go to the back of the village? It would have been faster to get here from the side; look the mountain is much lower and narrower here." Adimen's tone was still neutral.

"I didn't exactly have a map then . . . plus, remember, I didn't plan to get over the mountain and I didn't even know there was an 'over the mountain' until yesterday. I thought I heard the First Generation on the mountain so I was searching for them and trying to get a good view. I looked for more comfortable and higher terrain. By the beach, the mountain is steeper even if it is less high so it was more complicated, plus I would have been in full sight of everyone else."

"What made you think that you'd get a clearer view of the mountain from the mountain?"

"Well, because, err, I don't know, I was not seeing them from the ground so . . ." mumbled Indarra felling a little stupid.

"We were just trying to find our parents. That's a heroic action so don't make it sound like we did something idiotic," barked Tom who had been silent throughout the whole exchange.

"Well, no, I'm just trying to put the pieces together. I just don't think you see the mountain better from the mountain. I could be wrong but I don't think I am. Anyway, I'm asking all these questions because this is how you gather information. By cross-referencing the details we might find out something. Anyway, watch this, even though it's just a theory," she explained looking proud of herself. She pulled out another 3D model version of the village from the box. "If I add one of our villages to the two existing villages, we basically get a perfect circle, if we add the thickness of the mountain by the beach separating us obviously."

"Obviously!" Tom mocked but she pretended not to notice.

"This is what I've been working on all day; I tried to map out our two villages and understand what it would look like as a 3D model. And that's when I realized that our villages were each a 120-degree sector of a full circle."

Tom and Indarra looked more lost than when they had first found Robin.

"Let me explain it in a simple way. Here is a circle." She circled the three villages with her finger. "Let's say you found the center alright, like right here in the center in the middle of the mountain, then you cut it into 360 small slices; well, one village would be 120 of those."

"Or we could cut it into three and then still have three villages," said Tom dismissing the 360-degree thing.

"Well, circles have 360 degrees, that's just how it is, alright?" said Adimen coldly. She looked as if someone had just said that her child was ugly.

"OK, but how did you find the 360 slices without the third?" asked Indarra trying to calm the tension.

"It's very simple math," Adimen explained briefly how she did it, although neither of the Robatians understood but once they visualized it, there was no need for the math as the two villages were clearly two-thirds of a circle.

"I see it, but could it just be a convenient coincidence? I mean it just looks like a croissant if you don't stretch the mountain out at the back also. Also, we don't know that the mountain is that massive and what you think is the center of it could actually just be the back," said Indarra looking scared of Adimen.

"True. Either way, this is just a hypothesis. However, it's clear that combined we're still 240 degrees of a circle. That's a certainty, but it could be random."

"I think we all know it's not random and whether we spent days discussing it or not we're gonna go check out if there's a third village, right? So how do we do that?" asked Tom, suddenly feeling the soul of an adventurer.

"First, we need to find the most efficient route, and then pack up the things we need for it," said Adimen while fixing a small piece that came loose from the 3D map.

"Indarra, we—" Tom began but Indarra interrupted.

"I know; we can't just go on letting the twins think we're dead."

"That's a waste of time," said Adimen, back in robot mode.

"Going across that mountain really isn't that long, plus you wanna map out the place, right? The more you explore the better!" explained Indarra.

Adimen was well-read but Indarra had outsmarted her by understanding her personality and cornered her by appealing to her thirst for knowledge.

"We can't all go into the village so I'll go alone and meet you guys with the twins," said Indarra.

"What if people see you?" asked Tom, thinking he should probably propose to go instead of his friend but kind of chickened out of it.

"I'll tell them I hid in my house for a few days because I felt panicky or something."

The plan was simple. Indarra, Tom, and Adimen would walk back to Robat together. Once they neared the village, Tom and Adimen would set up camp while Indarra got the twins and then they'd walk over the mountain and walk down to whatever was in that missing third part.

"Alright, we wanna maximize the terrain exploration by walking a minimal distance and also minimizing risk-taking. I would say the path you guys used to get here was somehow the most efficient one. So, if we go through the middle, that is to say from the center of the back of the village, you have the least steep part but the distance is much greater. From the back corners of the village, like the barn or silo where you came from, it's steeper but still manageable, and the distance from one village to the next is shorter. Whereas the closer you are to the beach, the lower the mountain but we would need ropes to negotiate the rocks," explained Adimen.

"Why don't we just go around it from the outside, you know, from the water?" asked Tom.

"Coz none of us can swim faster than sharks! The arms of the mountain extend into the bay on every side; they go on for a good 100 meters after the coral bay and then slowly diminish into the water. We could climb around it but that would be really hard. This is how we'll proceed: we'll use the way you used to go to Robat. You and I will stop somewhere hidden half-way down into the Robat valley. Indarra, you'll walk down exactly as you got out, walk on the left road of the village down to the beach and into the twin's house. Once this is done, you meet us, and we will set out for the center of the island. From there we should get a view of the whole terrain since it seems like the center of that circle and if it is a circle, it would be the highest point. Then we will walk to whatever seems to be the new unexplored terrain and you know, study it!"

"When should we go? If we get there in the middle of the night, I can actually sneak in without anyone up and the twins will be home for sure! I say, we leave around three so we make it to base camp around roughly 7 PM. We can have dinner there and then I can head off around 10 as I'll still be able to see with the lights from the village. I get the twins and we head back. It'll probably be late by then so we can rest in base camp and then leave at sunrise."

"Great plan!" exclaimed Tom.

"It really is a great plan, but really, it is going to be complicated to carry everything in our hands like that though. We need food and I need to bring documents for field studies which means that if we fall we drop it all," said Adimen looking like the problem was unsolvable.

"We got that under control," said Tom proudly feeling useful finally. "You take fishing nets, make a knot here and there, and you wrap it around your shoulders so it dangles on your back. If you pack everything in the nets it's all on your back and your hands are free."

"Wow, that's very ingenious," she said and looked surprised.

"We came up with the idea! With the twins!" said Tom enthusiastically trying to make his moment last just a little longer.

"They're really lucky, to have friends who love them." Adimen looked away and started looking through her books compulsively with no actual purpose. After a long 30 seconds of total silence, she looked away from them and said, "The plan is great. I will make a 2D map that's far easier to carry than the 3D version but it's good we have it as we can calculate distances better on the 3D version. Then all I'll have to do is trace the trajectory on the 2D map and follow it. So, tomorrow, I'll head to work, work out the perfect path, then I'll get food for lunch and dinner tomorrow night and another two meals for four as we don't know how long we'll be gone for. How about water?"

"We did without it last time. I guess we could use the containers they use for food and hope the water doesn't spill but it will be heavy and uncomfortable. I say we do without it for the first journey and we'll bring some up from Robat to the camp as we can go seven hours without drinking. We'll bring enough for the night and we'll just have a little for the walk to whatever is on the other side. Plus, peeing on that mountain was not comfortable so I'd rather stay off the water," said Indarra, remembering her experience squatting on the uneven terrain.

"Great. OK, we should go to sleep now. We have a big day ahead of us tomorrow."

They all said good night and went to bed, although none of them could really sleep. Somehow, the sleeplessness was not about the adventure awaiting them the next day, but because they all had their own reasons to stay awake. For one person it was going back to that mountain, for another the excitement of seeing someone again, and an unusual feeling of accomplishment for the last one. The plan was simple, and nothing could or would go wrong. However, in the scale of their world, each square centimeter was like an ocean. Eventually, they fell asleep, though Adimen got up again to triple check the way she had chosen was the most efficient one. After a few frenetic calculations, she finally agreed her first choice was the best and she had found a great path that would be fast but also allow them to see slightly different territory from what the others had seen before. She was really worried about the second part of the journey beyond the peak of the mountain, as that would take her far away from what had been explored by her two new friends so far. What if walking towards the blank space in the circle led all of them to their deaths and she was responsible for that? As hardworking and determined as she was, her knowledge would not help her work out a plan for a place she had no information on so far.

In the morning, Adimen left for work as she said she would and came back with all the supplies they needed.

She had even taken into consideration Indarra's unusual food restrictions and brought a whole turkey and zucchinis to feed them all for a while. Indarra made the bags and even took care of the one Tom had attempted to make. He looked a little frustrated but his new passion for adventure kept his spirits high. Adimen put books in one of the bags and then weighted the bag, removed one, and then somehow added two more. Then she would walk back to a shelf and start browsing through a new book, empty the whole bag, and start the whole process again.

"So! You seem like a smart cookie, so maybe you know everything in those books already and you don't need to bring them?" Indarra suggested.

"Thank you, but no, I don't know everything. I'm just trying to figure out which books I'm the least familiar with so that I can bring it and use it later."

"We can't carry too much; I think water will save us more than the books if we're trapped somewhere," said Indarra trying to be gentle but sounding bossy instead.

"Well, maybe if we have the books we won't get trapped!"

"Alright! Let's go! The twins must be worried," said Tom, stopping what could have gotten ugly pretty quickly.

"Of course, let's go. Please don't take too many books, Adimen," said Indarra.

After another 20 minutes of failed attempts from Indarra to force close the book bag, they finally left. They turned left, walked the 80 meters that separated them from the right side of the Robin mountainside, headed to the back of the village towards the barn, and started walking up a slightly steeper side of the mountain than they had done previously. That is, they were maybe 100 meters closer to the ocean. Adimen said it was probably the most efficient way and would avoid redundancy in their trajectories. Indarra obviously thought it was bullshit but didn't say a thing. The walk was harder than before as it was steeper, but it was feasible. Adimen was surprisingly comfortable and seemed to be more in shape than Indarra thought she would be. It made her like her a little more but annoyed her a little for a reason she didn't really understand. After an hour or so, they could feel the gradient under their feet decrease until they finally reached flat land. Suddenly there it was: their home, Robat. The sight of her home made Indarra feel much better. Then they all turned around to see Robin disappearing behind them, which was an oddly uncomfortable feeling.

"I can't believe it!" said Adimen with her eyes shining. "It's beautiful! I've been working on the map, but somehow, I've been seeing it as a hypothetical project – not that I didn't believe you!" she added quickly. "It's just now I see it with my own eyes and the world I thought I knew . . ."

Indarra looked at Adimen. The strange girl from Robin wasn't speaking but literally thinking aloud, unfiltered, giving Indarra a glimpse of the raw Adimen. It was like she could see inside her for a brief moment and her emotions had turned her into an open book. She probably didn't even know she was speaking out loud. Her eyes sparkled with a mix of fear and thirst for more, but there was also sadness there. Indarra thought she looked beautiful and couldn't take her eyes off her. She somehow felt drawn towards her like a magnet and just held her hand as they stood there. Though Tom was right there, they were alone in the world for an instant, in this new world they had just discovered, a world that had doubled in the course of a day but somehow felt like it wasn't any bigger than the space under their feet.

Then Tom clumsily killed the moment. "So, we should walk a bit more before Indarra walks down to the village alone, right?"

"Err, yes, of course. Hmm, so we'll stop right there, one-third of the way to the village. We need to be high enough not to be spotted. Indarra, you're OK walking down there alone right?" Adimen asked, all business-like.

"Obviously. I've done it before and it will be fine."

They walked for another 20 minutes and set up camp where they'd wait for Indarra to come back with the twins. They had to wait a couple hours so Indarra would get there after dark and sneak into the house quietly and be sure of finding the twins there. They all watched the sun set over the bay as they unpacked their dinner and ate as if they hadn't eaten in days. The hike had made them hungry. Once the sun had totally set, Indarra headed down to Robat. It had only been two days but it felt like a lifetime. Maneuvering around the rocks in the dark wasn't easy and she almost fell a couple of times but made it down to the village OK. She could see the lights of the village shining brighter as she approached and suddenly, she was on flat land by the silo, right where she had been two days ago thinking she may never return. She walked down to the beach and made a left; the twins house was 100 meters from there but she didn't go there right away. Instead, she walked back to her house on the other side of the bay not knowing why but probably hoping that her family had somehow made its way back. Of course, they hadn't. She walked back to her room and found the note about the cycle of life her dad had written. She picked it up, folded it, and stuffed it in her pocket for no real reason and walked straight out of the house and back to the twins. The light was on when she got there and she could actually hear them laughing or arguing, either way, it made her feel so good to hear their voices. She didn't knock, she just entered. They were making dinner and Turk had tomato sauce all over his t-shirt.

"Hey, crazy!" said Ross and he threw a few peas at her.

Indarra took a seat around the bar and started poking at the pork ribs. "Man, that looks yummy, I hope you have enough for 3, then you can also cook something for you too!"

They all laughed and hugged Indarra.

"Where the hell have you been?" asked Turk, "We thought you guys died or something. We didn't know what to do. We thought about going to the mountain but then we thought, if it swallowed you up, well, then we would die too and you guys would be gone so what's the point. On the other hand, I thought that if it had eaten you and Tom it'd be full by now so we could maybe give it a go while it's digesting. Anyway, I guess just Tom was enough." He was joking but a glimpse of fear trailed into his voice. "Where is Tom?" he asked more seriously.

"Oh, he's fine, he set up camp an hour's walk from here with Adimen."

"Adimen?" they both asked.

"Yeah, she's that girl we met in the other village."

"The other village? What? Hold on a minute, what are you talking about?" Turk's eyes were wide open and looked like they were about to pop out of their sockets.

"Long story short, there's another village, just like ours, and I mean just like ours," she insisted, trailing on each syllable. "Their walls are different colors and their school is bigger, coz they didn't have you there so you know, they actually had to educate their entire population . . ."

"You, b—" started one of them but she stopped him and kept on going.

"There is, I think, the same number of people there and basically they're like us, only brainier and chubbier. Oh, we mapped out the place and it looks like there's a negative space – that's what she called it. Anyway, it looks like if this land was a circle and we put our two villages in that circle, we could fit a third one. This is when you guys pack up your shit and leave right now so we can all go together to find it, yeah!" she screamed in exaggerated excitement, wondering if they would actually come.

"Well, this is clear and simple, let's just go!" said Ross sarcastically. "Why do you even want to go to that other village?"

"I don't know! Curiosity? We don't know if there's another village there, but whatever's there, our world is bigger than we thought and we should explore it!"

"What if all that grows there are peas?" asked Turk.

"Well, I guess I'll just have to start eating you then."

"I can't believe you're alive," said Ross, really seriously for the first time. "We really wanted to go find you and we actually started going toward the base of the mountain yesterday but Deborah's regime kind of kept us from doing it . . . long story, but she's sort of in charge here now."

"I can't believe that! Actually, I perfectly can as she's a lunatic. Alright, we've wasted enough time. How about you pack up! Wait first give me a big glass of water and then fill some containers with water so the guys up there can drink. We also need to pack enough water so we have some for later."

"We can just use the jars we use for tomato sauce; it'd be easier," said Turk.

"Brilliant, you do that, and I'll go use your shower. Let's meet down here in 30, ready with the water."

It wasn't a surprise it was so easy to convince the twins to leave the village. It was a well-known fact that they were adventurous, reckless and, well, simply crazy. Indarra was a little worried about them being near Adimen as they were so different. Adimen was uptight, bossy, and annoying while they were . . . well, they were annoying too, but a different, fun kind of annoying. It would be fine, she thought, yep, they would have to be fine. An hour and 10 minutes later, after several rounds of screaming fits from Indarra, the twins were ready and chilled as always.

"Guys! I'm pulling you out of your home into what might be death; can you please pretend to be slightly nervous and concerned about the situation?"

Turk tried to shape a particular male body part into the sand, seemingly without a concern in the world.

"Hopeless!" she cried. "Let's just hit the road. It's not too far and don't worry, the mountain is safe."

Finding Adimen and Tom on a large dark mountain turned out to be harder than finding a well-lit village in the valley and they walked back a couple of times thinking they had gone too far. It turned out they hadn't, it was just harder to appreciate distances in the dark. However, after a few cries of impatience, they finally made it.

"Guys, please meet Adimen. Adimen, this is Turk and Ross, if you can't tell them apart, remember they're both idiots but Ross is slightly more stupid," Indarra said slapping him on the back of the head.

"It's so strange to be meeting more people. I still can't believe it!" said Adimen looking back and forth at her new friends and at her slightly less new friends. "Hi!" she said finally, not knowing what to do with her arms.

"Hi, well, we're meeting someone new this very second for the very first time in our lives so imagine how we feel!" said Ross.

"Oh, I remember, I met someone new for the very first time yesterday, in my bed!" she said looking at Tom accusingly, but with some complicity.

"Alright guys, we'll set up camp and spend the night here. Here is the water and some food. If anyone has to pee, please walk at least 100 meters away from here and yes, I'm not saying this for Adimen who I don't expect will drop her panties to her ankles two meters from here, I'm talking to you two!" Indarra pointed at them and frowned.

The twins laughed. "Yep that sounds like us," said one of them proudly.

They all ate and tried to get to know each other. This was an awkward experience since none of them had ever met anyone before. Everyone they knew, they had known since birth. The twins were surprisingly well-behaved but a little too curious. Adimen didn't seem to be very comfortable when they asked her about the pooping frequency in her village. She quickly changed the topic and tried to get more Intel about Robat's education system.

"It's not really a thing here you know," said Ross dismissively. "All you have to do is turn up occasionally and maybe, if you get in trouble, break into Indarra's house while she's busy helping out with underwater fishing, mostly on Tuesday afternoons, and get all the info you need about the homework."

"What? You wouldn't know where to find it!" laughed Indarra.

"Left drawer, under your diary." Ross paused for a moment for effect and added, "Sick pervert by the way!"

"Ross, I could kill you!"

The atmosphere was relaxed and everyone was getting along, but Indarra was genuinely upset about Ross reading her diary!

"So, Adimen, are you seeing anyone?" asked Turk casually.

"Keep it in your pants and leave her alone, she might not want to share her entire life in front of a group of total strangers," barked Indarra.

"No, it's OK, I don't have anything to hide. I don't have anyone back in Robin as I'm always very busy working. But I think Indarra is a beautiful and brilliant woman and anyone would be lucky to be romantically involved with her."

You would have expected most people, and Adimen above all, to blush for being so truthful about their feelings but she didn't. There was not a trace of shyness or anything. It was impressive.

"You're a really attractive woman too, Adimen, I must say and I'm surprised you're not involved with anyone," said Indarra looking her straight in the eyes.

"I'm single and handsome and attractive too!" declared Ross faking being hurt.

"Yes, Ross you're a total catch!" laughed Tom.

"Alright everyone, we have a long day ahead of us tomorrow so that's enough compliments for now. Let's sleep!" commanded Indarra.

They must have all been exhausted as not even the twins tried to keep the rest of them awake and actually went to sleep obediently. Indarra woke up in the middle of the night, a bit cold and nervous. She looked around and saw Ross sitting a little away from the rest of the group. She got up and walked over to him.

"Hey there, can't sleep?" asked Indarra.

"Nope, kinda used to beds," laughed Ross.

"Yeah, this isn't ideal, but it's only temporary."

"I know . . . Indarra? Do you think we'll ever go back?" he asked looking at her like a little child.

"Absolutely! Why wouldn't we?"

"I don't know. I have a feeling we won't, not because we're gonna die or anything. It's just, everything's been so weird lately, between our parents disappearing, and now there is the other village . . . I'm scared, Indarra. I wish things would go back to what they were. I don't want the adventure, I want tranquility. I liked what we had before. I miss my parents and I know Turk does too. We haven't spoken about it at all, but I know he does. I heard him cry in his room the other day. I've cried too," he said looking away, his voice barely audible.

"It's normal to feel this way. So much has changed. And, yes, what we had was comfortable, that's for sure, and we all miss our parents and what we had before. But . . ." she started hesitantly, measuring her words for what was coming next. "Ross, we've been lied to our whole life. This tranquility you miss, it was a lie, but I'm not and I'll always be there for you and Turk and Tom and Adimen now, OK?" She hugged him, giving him a light tender pat on the shoulder blade. They stayed like that in each other's arms for a few minutes and she could feel his heartbeat accelerating. "Alright, we should try to sleep anyway. It will be a long day tomorrow, huh? Maybe you're this much more sensitive and hormonal because you're lacking sleep!" she laughed.

"Oh, shut up, you monster," he smiled, a little embarrassed but knowing this was the only way he wouldn't feel awkward in the morning.

They both returned to the camp and lay down next to their friends.

Chapter 6

PINK IS THE NEW GREY

They all woke up with the sun, as there were no black-out curtains up on the mountain. They quickly gathered their things and headed to the very top of the mountain, under Adimen's commands of course.

"OK, I think we're only 30 minutes from the top of the mountain now," declared Adimen knowledgeably.

"You guys see that!" said Tom. "What is that?"

"I don't know, but it looks manmade," said Indarra.

"It's like a house but a weird, skinny, tall house with no walls!" said Turk amazed, trying to describe the unknown as well as he could. What they were approaching was an antenna; they had never seen one before, so a weird, skinny house with no walls it would be!

"Wow!" exclaimed Ross when they finally got to the antenna. "This thing is huge; it's like 10 times taller than our house. Why couldn't we see it before?"

"Well, because the mountain is steep and this is a flat area, so you'd hit an angle if you wanted to see it from the bottom," explained Adimen.

"Hmmm, guys, I think you need to come and see this," shouted Turk. He had climbed the ladder to the top of the antenna and found a platform around it. They all climbed to the top and just stared in amazement without saying a word for a full minute. They kept turning around on themselves. Even though they expected to find a third village, they were still surprised and amazed at this discovery. The view was incredible. You could see the whole island and the three arms of the mountain dividing it perfectly into three and then diving into the ocean. It was impossible to tell which village was which from a distance, as they really looked identical.

"I can't believe it; it's true there really are other villages!" said Turk as if he couldn't believe his own eyes.

"Alright, guys, I know the view is incredible, but we have to head down as soon as possible so we don't have to sleep on the mountain again," said Adimen, sounding almost jaded with their adventure.

"Correct me if I'm wrong, but if we can see the villages, then they can see us too," said Ross.

"I guess so, but it's so far that it probably just looks like another tree," said Indarra.

"Wow, I can actually see people walking around. I can't tell which village is which though, so how are we gonna know which is which now?" asked Ross.

"It's OK, the ladder was facing my village," said Adimen. "So, if Robin is at your back, your village is on the right and the third village is on your left, which is where we're heading. Alright, everybody start climbing down!"

The walk down seemed endless and Tom started complaining 30 minutes in. Adimen was clearly struggling but she suffered in silence, and the twins made fun of Tom as usual until Indarra snapped at them.

"Shut up, guys, you're being assholes as usual. If you weren't this busy being fools, maybe you would notice the village," said Indarra.

"Oh, shit man, it's super pretty. Why don't we get fun colors like this? All that grey . . ." said Ross grimacing.

"The school is like yours," said Adimen. "Smaller than ours, but they have another building by the fields and also by the beach with a large outdoor area which seems full of people. Hmm, interesting," she said insisting on each syllable.

This village was incredible; one house was pink with a purple roof, another one bright copper with a golden roof, and there were so many other colors. When they had almost finished their walk down, they could see everyone was on the beach and they hoped they would go unnoticed by the locals as they made their way. Our joyful group was going straight down the center of the village, between the silo and the barn.

"We should do it the way we did it the other time; just go left or right and go down between the rows of houses and then we quietly—"

"Hey! Dad!" screamed a voice.

They all looked to their right and saw a young man on the mountain, 300 meters away from them.

"Hey wait up, guys," the young man shouted as he ran toward them. "Dad!" When he drew nearer, he stopped, completely frozen, and his face changed.

For a long moment, they just stared at each other not knowing what to do, the same way you would bounce on your heels and toes and wonder if you should stay put or try to cross the road when the little guy goes from green to red on traffic lights.

Adimen stepped forward and started walking slowly toward him. "Hey, err, my name is Adimen, and we are not looking for trouble. We come from two other villages across the mountain and only found out about each other's existence two days ago after our parents disappeared. Are you looking for them too? Did they disappear? Is that why you were calling out for your dad?"

The boy started stepping back. He was terrified! His handsome face was so contracted it hurt just to look at it.

His body was strong and muscular but he now looked like a puppy with a broken leg.

"Please don't be scared," tried Indarra now advancing cautiously towards him as well. "My name is Indarra and that's Tom, Turk, and Ross. We come from the same village. We met Adimen two days ago when we got to her village and we've been friends since. We figured there could be a third village so we left last night because we really wanted to meet you and hoped you may have answers to what has happened. We're almost out of water and we haven't eaten in 24 hours. We slept on the mountain last night. Do you think we could stay in your village tonight and maybe get some food and water? We're really tired and can't make it back to our village without getting our strength back." Indarra was a very good judge of character and knew that by asking for a favor, she was putting him in a position of strength and the boy relaxed right away, but to be fair, knowing him, it was probably out of compassion.

The expression on his face changed as if he suddenly felt like he had lacked manners and should have welcomed his guests in a better way. "Please, of course!" he said apologetically walking towards them rather fast. "I'm sorry; I thought you were my parents and I just, I'm sorry." He was really confused and kept looking back at his village, then back at them, then at the top of the mountain.

"Sorry to ask, but were you guys on top of the mountain around 12?"

"Yes, we were," said Adimen.

"I saw you guys. I thought it was . . . well, our parents all disappeared a few days ago and you're gonna think it's crazy, but when I saw people on top of the mountain I thought it was them. I kinda tried to keep my eyes on you while you were coming down but I could not always see you so I decided to risk it and walk up here and that's when I bumped into you. So I guess that wasn't my parents up there after all," he said sadly.

"I'm really sorry," said Indarra, not putting a reassuring hand on his shoulder but sounding as empathic as she could muster. "Losing my parents is actually what got me up the mountain first three days ago and that's how I found the other village where Adimen comes from. Your parents disappeared in the middle of the night four days ago as well?"

"Yes, it was horrible; we all woke up in the morning and they were all gone."

He must have looked so sad; I wish I had been there to hug him then.

He looked down and said. "I think I'll never see them again."

They all looked at each other, unsure what to say or do. "What's your name?" asked Ross. Sometimes he wasn't too clumsy and this was one of those rare times.

"My name is Artea."

"Stop staring at him, you're gonna make him feel uncomfortable!" said Indarra to Turk as they walked towards the man's village.

"Sorry, but, I mean look at him! Argh, he is so annoying with his muscular arms, big full lips, his blue eyes, and blah," said Turk.

"Turk, stop it, try to be in love or jealous in silence for now. You can be off-putting to him like you are to the rest of us in a couple days when he knows you better," she laughed.

"OK, sorry, I'll look at your butt instead. It's pretty muscular but maybe a little too big . . ." Indarra looked at him offended but he continued describing her.

" . . .but the hips make up for . . ."

"Turk!" she snapped.

"OK, OK, I'll stop."

"So, what's the plan?" asked Adimen a little worried. "We can't just all burst into your village as if it was normal."

"Hmm, actually I think you can," said Artea. "My people will be surprised but really happy to meet you."

"Better than those weirdoes in the other village," whispered Indarra, elbowing Tom in the ribs in a partner-in-crime sort of way.

"Don't be bitchy, they just didn't know anything about us," said Tom in what Indarra termed a so-not-like-him-annoyingly-wise sort of way.

As they approached the village, its colors seemed more vivid. It was so unlike anything they'd seen before. As far as Robat or Robin, the only real colors they could see were the green of the flora and the blue of the sky and ocean. They were walking faster now as if this new place was welcoming them with its bright yellows and stunning pinks.

"So, you're Ross right?" asked Artea.

"Yes!"

"So, how come you have a copy of yourself?"

Ross laughed really hard. "It's called a twin. In our village, women sometimes have two babies at a time and that's what happens. It's rare but it happens. I think we're the only current twins alive. I heard prior generations had some. Anywho, we're two different people even though we look the same, sound the same, and have the same outstanding sense of humor. I'm a lot more handsome than my brother and I smell like I fell in a jar of roses at birth though. So yup, yup, yup, we're different people."

"You're very funny," laughed Artea. "Do you stare as much as he does? Where I'm from we don't stare as much."

"Hmmm, well, Turk and I don't answer to rules, whether they're social or otherwise. We're just above it. Indarra calls it being 'freaking immature assholes' but I call it freedom!"

"You guys have such strong tempers. Everyone in Robart is just," he paused thinking of the right way to put it, "very nice here, but they're not as edgy. I think I have this edge in me though, you hot . . . immature . . . butt . . . thing," he said tentatively as if he'd always wanted to say something like this but never could. He blushed deeply.

"Yeah, well, you're getting the best of us here. We're like the best of both villages, plus Tom," Ross mocked. "So, what's with all the colors? Robart was it?"

"What do you mean?"

"Well, your houses, they're like crazy colorful and your clothes too . . . why are your pants somehow going over your shoulders like this?"

"Oh, these are called overalls; it's nice when you're painting, so you don't stain your shirt."

"Painting? What's that?"

"Are you kidding?" asked Artea, his eyes wide open.

"No? Why?"

"How do you not know what painting is? What about sculpting?"

"Huh?"

"That's all we do around here and it's boring sometimes."

"But what is it?"

"Well, you have a white canvas and a brush and paint – that's a colored fluid," explained Artea when Ross made a confused face, "and then you paint pretty drawings on canvas."

"What is it for?"

"Don't ask me, I don't really get it either," he laughed. "But what else would we do all day anyway?"

"I don't know, like chill around!"

"Well, we chill while painting!"

I think that's when Indarra butted in and said something about chilling being his prerogative but not everyone else is where she was from.

The six of them came to a stop when the mountain leveled out, which literally happened within a distance of fewer than 10 meters. That's when they saw a big girl standing there with a basket full of peaches. She was sort of walking about with her basket as you'd do for a commercial for detergent with white sheets drying in the sun over a cornfield . . . She seemed to be talking to herself, or to the peaches, who could tell . . . And that's when she started spinning and spinning on one heavy leg, looking up to the sky. When she came to a stop, she saw Artea with the five strangers. You'd probably expect her to drop the basket and the peaches would roll over to stop at their feet as she screamed her head out running back to the village. However, she didn't do that and just said, "Hello there!"

"Berenice, don't worry, they're just . . ." started Artea not really knowing what to say.

"Why are your clothes monochrome?" asked the girl as if meeting new people for the first time ever wasn't what was the most striking at this very moment.

"What?" asked Indarra.

"How do you get the juices flowing? How does inspiration come from monochrome? On the other hand, do you like a neutral frame so that the colorful beauty of your imagination can ravish by standing out from the grey? That would mean that you're the frame of your work, but then I think I'm the heart of my work, though maybe my clothes aren't me so are they the frame? Or is my work the heart itself and I'm just its tool and my clothes the frame and I've been disrupting it by blinding it with such flashy overpowering colored clothes? I need to go change right away!" The girl disappeared.

"So that was Berenice; we do a lot of hmmm, that, here," said Artea a little embarrassed.

"Well, that wasn't so bad. Maybe she was just surprised and that was her way to cope with it, whatever she was saying," said Tom not convinced.

Meeting Berenice wasn't exactly reassuring to any of them. Sure she seemed harmless but she really pushed the creepiness to a whole new level. They did not use the side roads as they did when they were sneaking into the other village or back into their own. This time, they walked through Main Street. It was just like their main street, with the forum on the right if you were walking down to the beach. The only difference was the people had played paintball in their village, well, maybe not paintball, but you get the idea. They walked all the way down to the beach where the school was and made a left. Where you would have had a large stretch of empty beach in Robat, you had what must have been 80 percent of the village population. Some were standing behind canvas, painting, others were sculpting unrecognizable shapes, a boy was playing the harp under a palm tree, two others were keeping their sandcastle wet, which was actually a model of the village, and there was a group dancing and singing while being accompanied by a very tall young man playing a guitar. Another one seemed to be making furniture, but the most fascinating one was a young woman Artea identified as Tina who had a bunch of containers, a small flame here, and a tube there so it looked more like chemistry. She would have fitted into Robin with all the science enthusiasts if it wasn't for this little '*je ne sais* crazy', plus she looked super happy! She twisted a knob just to let a bit of liquid get out and closed it right away. The liquid went through some kind of filter and out of another tube and into a glass, which she sipped and said, "Good stuff! Could be a tad less sweet but it really hits the spot." She threw her head back in contempt and burped loudly. "Hey girl," she said to Tom handing him a glass. "Woooooow, this brew must be the best I've ever made, seriously try it, I can't even recognize who you are, wooooow!" She got up to get closer to the new visitors and tried to touch Adimen's face who kinda took a step back with an air of disgust and disapproval.

"Sorry to tell you that, Tina, as awesome a brewer as you are, I don't think these are the effects of the alcohol," Artea said.

"You mean that's the plant I made you breathe in last night? Could the effects really come such a long time afterward?"

"Hmmm, nope, these actually are new people . . . This is Tom, Indarra, Adimen, Turk, and Ross. Guys, this is Tina, and she's my best friend here," he said in a naive sweet way. "I told you I thought I saw our parents in the mountain this morning right?" he said to Tina.

"Yep, see! I told you it was the plant, you fool!" she declared proudly while swinging her concoction over her head.

"Well, no it wasn't the plant either, I found them on the mountain. They were walking down from up there."

"Are we like, not supposed to go there or we'll die in some atrocious way?"

"Yeah we thought so too," said Indarra. "Turns out we have been lied too by our parents or maybe it was generations ago but the lie went on for generations with no one ever daring to go up there."

By this time, everyone had noticed the newcomers and had let go of their instruments, brushes, clay, and manuscripts. None of them seemed really worried or aggressive and just stood there and stared at them. One of the dancers came over and introduced himself. His name was Phil and he wasn't even a dancer but just had a go at everything, like they all did in this village! Everyone was curious and none of them looked as surprised as they should. It was as if you had just told them that even though the forecast said it would rain tomorrow, it turns out it might actually just be overcast.

"Wow, man this is crazy! It's awesome, we are so bored in this dump, I'm glad there's more. You guys have any fruit we don't have?" asked Tina.

"Oh, you eat a lot of fruit?" asked Adimen.

Indarra listened, hoping she meant watermelons as large fruit worked in her diet.

"Eat fruit!" Artea laughed. "No way, Tina is not what you'd call the healthy type. She turns it into something that burns your throat and makes you feel loopy."

"You're making alcohol. Fascinating! Will you show me? You know you shouldn't drink it though. It's good for preserving ingredients and cleaning cuts," said Adimen knowledgeably.

"Well, I'm full of cuts in here!" said Tina triumphantly taking another swig.

"I don't think mental disturbance should be something done to ourselves on purpose," nagged Adimen.

"You guys must be starving, how about we get you settled?" said Artea breaking the tension.

"Yeah, actually I think first we're in bad need of a shower," said Indarra desperately. "Do you have a free house for us to shower?"

"A what?"

"A shower! How do you guys wash?"

"In a shower, in the village bathroom. What's a house?"

"Well, it's like a building with bedrooms and bathrooms and a living area and a kitchen."

"You guys don't eat together?" asked Artea.

"We do."

"So you all bring your own food that you cooked beforehand?"

"Nope."

"Then why do you have kitchens in your err . . . houses?"

"Yeah, that's a good question that we never really figured out; they just come with one. Maybe if a group wants to separate itself somehow but I don't know."

"And you have a room to live in? As in being there all alone? Separated from the rest? What do you do there?"

"I don't know! Rest, read!"

"Can't you do those things in a communal space?"

"I guess so. I guess our villages are very different."

"They really are. It sounds fascinating, I can't wait to explore and see your habits and those houses you talked about. We have a lot of empty bungalows here since our parents left so feel free to pick whatever room you want. You have this one and two over there and . . ." Artea started showing them the bungalows.

They picked out three on the beachfront for Turk, Tom, and Indarra, while Ross and Adimen were in the second row. Indarra picked a room that was on the extreme right of the village if you were facing the mountain, just a few meters from where her house was in Robat. As Robart was on the right side of Robat, she was as far as possible from her old house and yet it somehow felt right. She stepped into her little bungalow with its slanted roof. It was spaced a couple meters from the next one and all were painted in different colors and style, but the same size.

Indarra's made me think of a Balinese bungalow. The outside walls were blue with a brown roof made of crafted wood. The double doors both had two heavy handles dangling into the shape of a, well, they'd call it the fat man . . . Inside was a beautifully crafted four-poster bed with light drapes that seemed to float magically around it. The room had hardwood floors, an armchair, and a large wardrobe. The walls were the same as the outside of the house. It was weird for Indarra not to have a bathroom, but the beauty of the room sure made up for it. She did not know what to expect of the bathroom and when she left the room she bumped into one of the Robartians.

"Oh, hi there, you must be Indarra, huh? It's so nice to meet you! Let me walk you to the bathroom. You guys must be in great need of clean warm water!" said the young man with a big smile on his face.

"Yes, we haven't showered in two days as we slept outside when we walked across the mountain. You have a beautiful village! What's your name?"

"I'm Victor, I'm in charge of the bathroom, and I'm the movie director!"

"The, err . . . the what?"

"So, you guys each have your own bathroom where you're from? That's incredible; I guess I would be out of work there!"

They walked through another row of bungalows. "So, as you see, the bathroom is behind the houses for convenience and only a minute stroll from your room! You walk the three rows of bungalows, and there you have it!"

Calling it a bathroom really was an insult as it was more the size of a small domestic airport terminal. You wouldn't say Robat was ugly and the houses were actually pretty luxurious, but there was something very clinical about them and an air of minimalistic luxury. Robart was a golden statue away from being tacky but remained in the tastefully extravagant category by a thread. The whole place was made of stones stacked on top of each other like in old temples to form beautiful arches, pillars, and fountains. Plants seemed to grow around them in a random but organized manner at the same time. There were stone animals here and there that looked like they'd been there for centuries! At least that's the look the place was meant to have. It was strange how everything was so colorful in the village but the bathhouse was made of bare grey stones. The flowers and plants made up for it though. Once inside, the grayness was over and you were back in Robart; there were thousands of small tiles of different sizes, shapes, colors, and textures. The first room was like a lobby with a fountain in the middle and the water was spraying out of a 'large lizard with wings'. On the left was a large room with shower heads sticking out of the ceiling and at the back were rooms with individual showers in case privacy was needed. Toilets were individual rooms on the left side of the building; basically behind the wall of individual showers but the doors to them were on the outside. Back in the lobby, was a huge arch that led into a steam room that could easily fit everyone from Robat, Robin, and Robart inside. Finally, on the right was a gym. You could tell dietary habits were good in all three villages. Some here had a bit more body fat than some people in Robat, but they basically all fell into the slim fit category. Tom and a few others had a few extra kilos, but calling him chubby would be pushing it. *Where I'm from we would call Tom beefy, but beefy was fat in those three villages.*

Robart was organized very differently from Robat. All the villages had three roads that went inland; the main road was in the middle and there were two side roads on each side but all three led to the barn, silo, and fields. Then there were streets parallel to the beach, which they called west-east, as if the north in each village was toward their side of the mountain. They all had two or three rows of houses or bungalows going back from the beach. Robart only had them east of Main Street, while the other two villages had them on both sides. However, the other two had fewer houses west of Main Street as the school was here on the beachfront with the forum behind it and the roundhouse on its left followed by the agricultural related buildings at the back before the land rose towards the mountain. On Robart, it was really different. They had three rows of bungalows on the beachfront east of Main Street and the bathhouse was located behind these. West of Main Street, beachfront, was the school and an outdoor cinema to its left, although a roof could slide over the cinema if needed. Behind sat a large movie studio, the forum, the roundhouse, and then the silo.

Indarra walked into the shower room. Though modesty was never actually taught in Robat you never had a reason to be naked in front of anyone as you had your own shower. People would sometimes swim naked but most of them would keep their underwear on, undress and get straight in the water, and then put their clothes back on. However, as there was no public naked body rubbing in Robat it was a little bit weird for her to see Tom, Adimen, Ross, and Turk all naked in that room. She hoped Tom felt alright about it. They had individual showers at the back but none of them were using them perhaps because they had not noticed them yet. She took off her clothes and put them on a bench near the entrance of the room where her friends' clothes were lying; stained with the filth of two days of intense walking. She walked to one of the shower hoses and turned the water on. The warm water felt great against her skin; not only was the filth being washed away but also the stress of those past few days and maybe somehow what she felt was the betrayal of so many years. The twins were obviously being fools, throwing shower gel at each other and mocking Tom.

"Soooo, this place is unusual," said Indarra kind of testing the water to see what her travel companions thought about it.

"It's awesome. Robat is a shit hole, I'm staying here. You get to stare at everyone naked on a daily basis!" said one of the twins, probably Turk.

"Are we like . . . settling here?" asked Tom with a trail of anxiety in his voice. "I mean, there are three villages, so how does it work now? Do we just pick the one that fits better? Return to the one we're originally from or do we just stay in this one coz that's what we're doing now?"

"I guess we get to choose as I don't believe being born somewhere entitles you to the place any more than the time you've spent there or anything. Of course, if there are no free houses, we can't kick them out, but with the population diminishing so drastically these past days, I don't think it would be an issue, above all here," said Indarra while trying to get the dirt out from under her toenails.

"What do you mean, 'above all here'?" asked Ross.

"Well, the math is easy, there's about the same amount of people in each village, right? Except there is far less housing in our villages. Look, unless Second Generations make the active decision to move out of their own house to move in with a friend, the disappearance of the First

Generation doesn't free up the houses where we're from. As it turns out, some people have moved in together, but this frees up like four houses in both villages. Here alone, about eight rooms were freed the second the First Generation disappeared."

Adimen looked at Indarra and nodded with respect.

"Your point being?" asked Tom.

"I don't know if I really have a point, just, well, if total freedom is allowed then how will we decide? What if four people want to move to your village and none of them want to live together but you only have two houses? What would happen?"

"It could be first come first served?" said Ross.

"Or priority to those who are OK sharing a house?" said Indarra.

"Maybe there could be a system of priority. For instance, if there are two people and one house, priority goes to the one who comes from the village, and if they come from the same one then maybe they take a test about the village and see who fits better," said Turk.

"This just there, none of these ideas are stupid, but who will decide which is more appropriate? There's no way one option will satisfy everyone."

"Or, we just tell them everyone else is dead and the villages were destroyed so there's no point going anywhere and we just stay here forever. That way we can all be happy and avoid the anarchy that will obviously come out of this decision making," said Adimen flatly.

"Hard stuff," said Turk. "I don't think that's our right to do that to all of them here or back in our villages, plus if they ever find out we lied . . . we're . . ."

"Maybe," interrupted Adimen, "but by telling them the truth, we're dooming them to a terrible end. I ensure you it will be chaos, although it might already be chaos if they each stay in their own villages."

They all dressed after their shower in the clothes the Robartians left for them on a bench and headed out of the bathroom. The sun was starting to set on the left flank of the mountain. This took some getting used to as it set over the ocean in Robat. It was probably around dinnertime by then, so they walked straight to the forum where all the Robartians were gathering to have dinner. It was a beautiful day, so everyone was eating upstairs but they still had to get their food from the ground floor. Today was chicken stir-fry, which worked for Indarra now she had finally agreed that chicken was a very reasonable size, bean sprouts aside obviously. However, she came to the conclusion she couldn't start fishing them out one by one and as they wouldn't be able to serve them to anyone else if she did it was better she eat them herself. When traveling, one needed to compromise, and if Turk could go a whole hour without harassing anyone, she could eat bean sprouts.

"Hey there guys, I'm Jerry, it's really nice meeting you. I'm the cook/server here with my brother Perry," said the man handing them plates.

"Jerry and Perry?" laughed Turk. "We're twins and our parents still found the will to give us drastically different names."

"Yeah, I'm not sure what happened here," said Perry. "All their inspiration must have been focused on something else. Anyway, it's chicken stir-fry today. I hope you guys like cilantro," he said without noticing Indarra's face.

Yes, it was small, and it bothered her but above all, she really hated it. Did you know that four out of 14 people hate cilantro? This dislike is not the way someone not used to eating fish can get a taste for it by having it more often, nope, some people's DNA makes the herb taste like dirty coins, cat piss, or soap, and there's nothing one can do about it to make it better. Most twins shared their likes and hates, however, Turk and Ross were part of the majority who liked cilantro and would have the pleasure of watching Indarra's torture.

"I don't mind, but we have a picky eater here," said Ross pointing at Indarra.

"Please, I don't wanna be a problem. I'm sure it's great!" lied Indarra guiltily, while giving Ross an icy look.

"Oh, I'm sorry, you don't like cilantro," said Perry. "Don't worry it's only sprinkled on top of your dish at the last minute so we won't put any on yours."

That's when the twins started explaining to the cooks Indarra's principles about not eating small entities and thereby minimizing the number of living things needed to feed the population.

"Wow, don't tell me!" said Perry. "I have that thing too, which my brother disagrees about so we compromise. I wanna avoid eating creatures such as artichokes or crabs as I think that if less than 50 percent of the creature is edible, then it shouldn't be eaten. We've been making stir-fries, soups, and salads out of broccoli stalks."

Indarra listened to him as if she was hearing someone say something smart for the first time in her entire life. At the same time, she started to think that maybe she could incorporate his diet into hers and she was thrilled.

"I wanna work for your kitchen!" Indarra almost screamed. "We would be a perfect fit; we could design menus that incorporate both our dietary rules and try to accommodate everyone while trying to maximize the use of products. We can stop peeling cucumbers and system-atically make pies or something with livers and all . . . I know that there can't be too many people working the same job, but maybe we can diversify. I'm a great fisher and diver, so I could fish in the morning, and still paint or something with you guys in the afternoons as this seems to be what you guys do. However, right after fishing in the morning maybe at like 10.30 AM, I could help you design meals for the day and even cook them partially if I have some time. What do you think?"

"Hey! We're the cooks in our village, so if someone should work in the kitchens it should be us!" said Turk.

"As it turns out, Jerry is only helping me because we're terribly understaffed in the forum. In fact, it's just me so far. My brother should have become a doctor at the transition so we're lucky no one has health-threatening diseases right now or gotten hurt, however, he still needs to prescribe medications for Asthma and other mild conditions. We're really overworked here. It would be perfect if he could go back to his full-time job. Even now, the two of us are clearly not enough to feed everyone on Robart but with the five of you here now, we would need at least three people working here, so you're all hired. The twins can work here full time, cooking and serving, I will be in charge of stocks and also cooking, while Indarra can fish, prepare menus for the following day, and eventually help out with the cooking when she can."

They were thrilled. Everything was going great, the people in Robart were lovely, and they seemed to have found their places in only two hours. They all took their food upstairs and sat at a table were Artea was sitting with Tina. They explained their new jobs and Artea seemed very excited. Tina was a little bit busy trying to force Tom to try each different type of liquor she had brewed in the past two hours.

⁂

"Food in Robat really sucked. How did we not realize it then?" said Turk with a mouthful of that delicious baked potato cheesy thing. "Indarra, you have to admit it, this is so much better than the crap you were fighting for; And the drinks! And everything here, look at this out there, how did we live without all this before?"

"Calm down. If you eat too much, you're gonna make yourself sick!" I said, knowing Turk's tendency to excess.

"I'm not a child! I'll make myself sick if I want to!" Turk took another defiant mouthful of the delicious dish. "So, what's for dessert? Can we have that weird brick thing with the chocolate on it?"

"He's right, Turk," said Indarra all mother-like. "You've had enough!"

"And stop drinking so much," added Tom.

"He's been badgering us for as long as I can remember about these songs; if you fall asleep or worse, you're gonna hear about it for a long time," added Artea.

"Oh, come on, I didn't speak about it that much!" I lied.

"Just be my ride!" They all started singing together and laughed while giving each other looks of complicity.

"Damn it, Indarra! Will you have the freaking duck thing already? They're the size of a chicken and that's reasonable! Besides, your miserable look is killing my buzz," said Turk.

"That's not the duck, Turk, I just feel bad having this much fun when—"

"You stop this right now, Indarra, you need to stop beating yourself up for being happy. Let's all smile and enjoy this incredible evening and then we'll head out!" said Adimen exasperated.

"I really really have to pee!" said Indarra putting her hands to her crotch.

"You're the sexiest thing alive," mocked Turk.

"Oh, whatever, just wait a minute. I'll be quick," said Indarra getting up from her chair.

"Front to back!" screamed Turk while she walked away.

She turned back to give him evil eyes while the group almost fell under the table laughing, trying not to vomit up their heavy dinner.

Chapter 7

AND . . . ACTION!

"I think this is going to be great for you guys. Perry is a great guy and you'll have a fantastic time working with him. The same goes for you, Indarra; this is going to be very fulfilling. Also, you'll get to meet Jack. He was a bit busy with the fishing but we couldn't justify the need in fish by creating a second full-time job, so you doing it as a part-time is perfect. We're still reorganizing here. With the First Generation gone, it has been a bit of an adjustment but it seems like everything is falling back into place and you arriving here seems to be working out perfectly. The more we are, the easier it is to somehow get the right dispatch of tasks," said Artea smiling at his food.

"What do you do?" asked Turk, giving him his prettiest smile.

"Err," he started answering blushing slightly, "I'm a farmer. I always loved growing things, it relaxes me, more than art. This is my art. I make nothingness turn into living things and feed my people with it."

"Oh, shut your stupid face with your blah blah," stammered Tina crawling out of her drunken stupor. "He's just being very modest; this hot piece of ass here is not only a sexy, muscle–coated, macho farmer, he has also helped all of us here find our place since the First Generation left. This is the only reason why there hasn't been anarchy here. He has this way of talking to people and of listening to them. He always finds a way to compromise. The bulge in his pants probably helps him too, you know, to get people to agree with him if you know what I mean. Grr . . ." and she tried to pull some sort of sexy clawing, you know, like a lion. It wasn't really sexy though. She could somehow speak pretty clearly for someone who had these many drinks in her. "So . . . I wanted to be a naked statue, you know, just standing on the beach every morning, for the moral of the population," she said casually, "but he convinced me otherwise with his deep blue eyes. So now, I organize the silo and I clean common spaces. I really got screwed over by his prettiness, huh! Oh, I'm kidding; I actually really like my job."

"How about us?" asked Tom pointing at Adimen then himself.

"Hmm, I'm not sure; I sure wouldn't mind the help in the fields and the company! So, let's see, what are you guys more comfortable with? I see you guys from Robat seem pretty fit. Tom, how about you give fitness classes on the beach, or in the movie studios if the weather is bad, in the mornings? If you see us in pairs and divide your mornings into four sections of one hour, you can see each of us for an hour every three days or so. And Adimen?"

"Well, I can help in the fields if you like. I can harvest and help you improve your growing cycle by studying the soil and create a fertilizer. Also, I'm good with electricity and everything related to electronics so I can fix things around."

"Perfect, how about afternoon activities? Are you guys more into acting, directing, sound editing, painting, sculpting, dancing, or singing?" asked Artea with confidence.

"It seems like this is more your specialty here, but we're eager to learn," said Indarra.

"Well, there's no rush as we're all better at some things but this is our entertainment here. We have exhibitions, we hang paintings, display statues and other work of arts, and we enjoy it in the evenings after dinner. It's a nice way to spend time together and talk about it." He went on explaining after noticing their uncomprehending looks. "But, the main thing here is the cinema, in which we all participate."

"What's cinema?" asked Tom with curiosity.

"Well, we have this machine which captures images that we can project onto a wall and watch. We have actors—that's us pretending to be other the people in it—and then there are props, décor, stunts, the music we include in it, and the special effects. There are practical ones with illusions or CGI, which means Computer Generated Images. For these, we modify reality with a computer and make it look different or we put two images on top of each other or remove something that shouldn't be part of it. It seems like this is where you could help, Adimen. Alright, speaking of which, we are going to show our last movie tonight. Oh, cinema is the craft, a movie is each individual piece," he explained as if telling them the air was going into their noses when they breathed.

After dinner, everyone walked to the cinema, which was on the beach. The whole complex was gigantic. Its footprint covered almost a third of everything that was West of Main Street. The complex included the indoor and outdoor studios and the cinema by the beach. Everyone sat on blankets on the beach. Tina had brought her brewing equipment for the occasion and was sharing it happily with everyone, except for Adimen who disapproved quietly. The movie started with an incredible view of Robart from the sky, but it looked a bit different to today. You could, of course, recognize everyone from Robart in the movie but they were playing the role of their parents. It seemed like it was happening when the Second Generation was about 10 years old. There was no 10-year-old there currently so they had to use shadows to pretend they were children and you would only see them from the back. Suddenly, the water receded in the ocean and a huge wave washed upon Robart. There were a few deaths, apparently among the children, as two of them were taken by the water. It ended with the reconstruction of the village and showed how if you stuck together, there was nothing you couldn't overcome. It was rather dramatic and kind of annoyingly cheesy but they had done a great job considering they were such a small team. When the movie ended, everyone walked to the studios, which had a door at the back of the cinema.

Victor approached the newcomers to inform them about the program. "Sometimes we just watch old movies, but it is a special day when the movie is screened for the first time and very exciting for all of us. This one is historical, but some are funny or in the Sci-Fi genre, however, whatever we do, after the first screening we all go and discover how it was made. We look at the movie set, see the tricks we used to make it all possible, and the costumes. Alright, let's go!" He waved them on to approach the door of the studios.

Tina was bothering some short boy, telling him how, at some point, movies had been all about being visually impressive, but they had no depth. The boy tried to escape from her with even more strength than he had from the wave in the movie. They walked in and they saw a replica of the village; it was enormous, the roof of the bungalows was knee-high.

"Good evening, everyone, whether you're from this place or another, I would like to welcome you to the BRS, known as the Bad Robart Studios! We're all really proud of this movie and we have all worked on it in different ways, so I would like to thank the actors, sound editors, musicians, scenarists, CGI specialists, stunts, and everyone who made this dream possible. I hope you enjoyed the movie and now, the magic continues with our special, 'The Wave, Behind The Scenes!' We used this model for large angles in which you could see the whole village or large portions of it. This room could be flooded with a water system bringing water from the sea. The whole set could be lifted and replaced with other sets such as full-size bungalows replicas for shots with the actual actors. We could fit up to three bungalows at a time here, a two-thirds version of the forum, and a third of the studios or the bathrooms, which we did! Now step back and admire the show!"

Everyone walked onto a stage at the back of the room and watched the sea retire from the beach to leave a dry ocean floor. Then, a dam suddenly opened and water rushed back into the bay and partially destroyed some of the houses, and flooded every road, house, and field until it crashed into the mountain. It then slowly started going back into the ocean taking trees, debris, and most of the beach with it. After a full minute of people in the audience screaming in enthusiasm, he pushed a few buttons and the whole set went up into the ceiling and a new one appeared with the bathroom. It was a pretty impressive movie set as the building was really large as a one-third version of the real one. They flooded it. Then they moved onto indoor scenes with buildings with three walls where you could see the different camera angles. Finally, the CGI specialist showed how he had added the sky and the mountain, and managed to include people in scenes where they couldn't possibly be for their own safety.

Artea was right; it really was an amazing way to bond with everyone. Even though they had their morning activities figured out, it really seemed that time here was cut into three parts. They did what was necessary for the good of the community in the morning and then do fun things in the afternoon and finally socialize in the evenings.

"Hey there! My name's Phil. Artea told me to find you. He said we could use your input with the technical aspects of movie making as you know your way around those things. I would love to hear everything you have to say about the movie, improvements you think we could make, and things you would had done differently. I wanna know it all!" said the overly enthusiastic man who had just walked up to Adimen.

"Oh, hi! Yeah, of course!" said Adimen a little surprised. "Well, hmmm, it was brilliant. I mean, I can't compare it to any other movies but I loved it. The visuals were breathtaking and it really looked like, well, you know . . ." she paused. "It brought back memories because it felt close to the truth. For the sake of making things easier for the team, I think I would have used unsalted water. I understand you want to stick as close to the truth as possible but you may want to reuse the set a few times for reshoots as salty water tends to damage things even once it's dried. It changes colors and your village is really colorful. Also, I don't think you want the water to start foaming before it hits shore as the wave was a perfect still blue and only started getting messy once it had reached us. I do understand you want the wave to arrive with a certain force, but just dropping it on a tilted slide would have been enough. Even if it was almost vertical you wouldn't get friction upon hitting the sea floor so you wouldn't get the foam. And last, I think you dumped too much water. The wave came from the side and didn't flood all the way back to the fields, it went a bit behind the forum and then stopped."

"Oh, so you guys had it too! That's impressive. Actually, here it hit us from the front and it did flood all the way back to the mountain, however, your points are fascinating. I'm really looking forward to working with you. Our next project will be called 'A Space Odyssey' and will be about other people living on land in the sky and interfering with one another. It will require some pretty hardcore CGI which I hope you can help with."

The twins were apparently about to make their debut as movie stars. The fact that they were twins was already something pretty special and, to be honest, their personalities and absolute lack of shyness would sure come in handy in the film industry.

After an incredible day that seemed more like a lifetime, they all went back to their room for a well-deserved night's sleep. A few days ago, the excitement and fright from all this change would have kept them awake, but this time, nothing could keep their minds' active. They were exhausted and passed out instantly on their beds.

In the morning, Indarra woke up starving. Back in Robat, they would return to their houses in the evening with food for breakfast, which they all ate separately in their own houses. However, she realized she didn't get anything last night to take away. Instead, they had gone to the cinema after dinner and to bed a bit later than she usually would. Also, she had no shower in her room so she couldn't get ready. She felt a bit confused at how a lifetime of habits had changed, and, above all, when she was still sleepy. Then she heard noises outside and figured people were up, so she dressed and walked out of the bungalow. Tom was talking and laughing with a boy by the beach and she was thrilled to see him so happy. He was also wearing the same clothes as last night, which made her believe he hadn't showered yet either.

"Morning, Ind, did you sleep OK?" asked Tom enthusiastically.

"Like a baby. It was amazing and I feel so rested."

"Let me introduce you to James. He's a movie set designer and basically built the whole set of the village for the movie yesterday."

"Hi there, nice meeting you," said the tall skinny man.

They had seen everyone yesterday since there wasn't that big a crowd but hadn't spoken to everyone yet – that wouldn't take long though.

"So, we bumped into each other two minutes ago here," explained Tom happily. "Turns out we're neighbors and we both snore . . . Anyway, he told me about his afternoon job and it just seemed like the obvious fit for me. I wanna design the sets with him. Doesn't it sound fun?"

It might have sounded like a question but the only possible answer to this was an enthusiastic nod from Indarra.

The three of them walked to the forum. When they arrived, they found a bunch of bags on a table downstairs. They each took one and walked upstairs where they found Adimen sitting with Artea. The twins were probably still asleep. Jerry and Perry were up, sitting at a table with a good-looking man with tanned skin, blue eyes, and very dark hair. They all greeted each other and sat down. Indarra opened her bag and found an orange, nuts, and a ham and cheese sandwich inside. There was a coffee dispenser in the corner, so she walked over to it and poured three cups. It was an uneventful breakfast and they just chatted about random things. Indarra found out Artea had received the farming gene from his mom and that he might have liked movies, but he wasn't that great at painting and sculpting but liked being very active. He was really surprised nobody did anything after dinner in Robat. A few minutes later, the twins arrived together. Even though they did not share a house anymore they were still perfectly synchronized. Then Perry got up and walked up to Indarra's table with the good-looking man.

"Hey guys, I'd like you to meet Jack. He's going to be your fishing partner, Indarra. You will be helping him from 8:30 AM to 10 AM every morning, then you can go shower and be in the kitchen from 10:30 AM till lunch time." Perry tried not to sound bossy. "We'll see if this works or if we need to give more time for one or the other. You can, of course, adjust it as you wish; whatever feels better, alright? I'll let you guys head downstairs and Jack will show you around."

After a few awkward exchanges and furtive looks towards one another, above all towards Jack from most of the newcomers, Indarra and Jack walked out of the forum and down Main Street to the beach.

"So, all our fishing equipment is in the shed by the school. We use nets, harpoons, and fishing rods," Jack explained. "First, we'll set the fishing rods on the rocks at the back left end of the bay and we'll set up the nets nearby. Then, we'll just harpoon bigger fish around this area and bring them back to shore while keeping an eye on the nets and the fishing rods, alright?" asked the handsome man.

"So, Jack, are you as fascinated by the underwater as I am or is it just a job? I used to explore every part of our bay as a kid, well, the parts I could reach . . ." Indarra tried to break the ice and connect with her new coworker, but somehow, it seemed to come across as her accusing him of not being as professional as she was.

"Yep, I like it down there," said Jack without any detail.

"Oh, great, well, then we'll get along for sure! Did you get to meet the other four?" asked Indarra with a happy engaging voice trying to make eye contact with Jack.

"Not really." He was still looking towards the horizon.

"Oh, OK, well, there's plenty of time. I'm sure you will all get along just fine, they're great people. And so are you, all of you here, in Robart, I mean. We've been welcomed beyond our expectations. Thank you."

"OK, get the rods and stick a rock on them so they won't move."

Indarra felt like she had just opened her heart to someone and that in return the recipient was like, 'Great, now here is an empty yogurt cup, dispose of it as you wish.'

Without further ado, Jack dove in the water and disappeared. Indarra fixed her mask and followed quickly after him. She had missed the feeling of quietness, the light you got down there, and the colors. They were just incredible and she realized the Robartians must have been inspired by the reef when they designed their village. Jack did not seem very friendly or eager to make friends with her, but she didn't care. If anything, it was probably better as Robart seemed to have a way more communal way of living than she was accustomed to, so, having those two hours to herself every morning to swim, relax, and think about what she wanted was probably all she needed. That morning, she did not really fish as all she wanted to do was swim and discover the bay. If she came back to the surface to breathe while Jack was outside carrying a fish he had just harpooned or handling the rods and the net, she could notice his looks of annoyance. He probably thought she was lazy, but she didn't care about it much. After all, they had been through, she deserved a moment to herself. Besides, she thought that it was already great that she was working two jobs 16 hours after arriving in the village. That was pretty quick integration. After trying to brush a particularly small fish with her hand, she lost it and ran out of air so she broke through the surface to catch her breath. She saw Jack wave at her and thought 'he's friendly after all' so she waved back. However, it turned out he was just trying to get her attention.

"Hey, Indarra, it's a two-person job OK? I can't be in the water and handle the nets and the rods at the same time. Well, actually I will once you're gone in like 10 minutes, but while you're here, these things have to be handled by the two of us," said the man flatly. He didn't yell or sound emotional, but his people skills weren't great.

"Oh, I'm sorry I . . ." started Indarra but Jack jumped straight back into the water without giving her a chance to reply. She thought it was really inconsiderate of him to talk to her that way when she was so new here. She deserved a couple days of adaptation if not at least half a morning! She knew what she had to do; there was a place only she knew about where she could get the largest fish, which of course worked out really well for her diet. She started swimming away towards the center of the bay. Jack started screaming in protest as he probably thought she was leaving early. Then she took in as much air as she could and dove straight down like a stone until her head started hurting from the pressure. She swam towards what was the deepest part of the bay where there was a squared black shadow at the bottom in Robat, and, as it turned out, there was here too. She couldn't reach it as it was too deep, but when you got close enough it felt like there was an underwater cavity, as the land folded in around her. The largest fish hid at this depth. Her head started throbbing and her vision blurred from the lack of oxygen but she couldn't come up without a fish. She was getting desperate and knew the risk she was taking was not worth it just to make a stupid point, but her oxygen-deprived brain couldn't function well enough to make a good decision. That's when she saw it, deeper towards the squared black shape. She gave one jerk with her legs and harpooned the 45 kg tuna. The animal died on the spot. She grabbed it and started to head back up as quickly as she could. She did not look up as she knew she was still really deep and didn't want to get discouraged by the distance left she had to swim. She could have let go of the fish to go faster but she would never waste a dead creature and did not want to return to Jack without it. Although, if she didn't make it up there would be two dead creatures who would remain uneaten. When she felt like she was going to pass out and that the tuna was going to slide out of her arms, the light changed and she thought maybe she had died but then she finally broke through the surface of the water. Jack must have noticed she had been underwater for a really long time because he was swimming towards her. She was out of breath and not going to be able to breathe normally for a few minutes. He was getting closer, but she did not want him to notice that she was in distress, however, the more she tried to control her breathing the more it became out of rhythm.

"Let me help you with that. That's an incredible catch," said Jack impressed and showing some kind of emotion for the first time so far.

"Nope, I'm good, thank you; this is what I always fish and I'm used to it. This is how I fish," she said exasperated.

She dragged the tuna back to the rocks. She struggled to bring it back as it was bigger than what she was used to even though it was true she always caught larger fish than other people. However, she was not going to ask for help from Jack. Besides, if he got closer to her, then he would hear her desperately gasping for air and she was not going to give him this satisfaction. After a while, she finally felt the rocks underneath her feet. As she started getting out of the water she tried to pull the tuna out with her but it was so heavy her fingers poked through its skin. The gooey flesh was repulsive. After a few different attempts, she somehow managed to wrap her arms around it. She finally got hold of it, carried it with what she tried to make look like ease, and dumped it next to the other ridiculously small fish. The other 12 fish together had less meat on them than this single tuna. She walked away proudly, with tuna blood running down her arms and flatly said, "Bye, Jack."

She could have walked around back to the beach but she decided she would swim it as she wanted to wash the tuna off her and not cross the whole village smelling like a tataki left in the sun for too long. She swam back and saw Tom in the middle of a cardio workout with Jerry and Phil. They were doing jump squats and it seemed like Phil was trying to show off by over doing every single move . . . She did not walk too close to them as she did not want to disturb Tom's class but they made eye contact as she walked out of the water. He winked at her and it felt good. Robart's waters might have some dark energy, but back on land, everything was back to its happy atmosphere. She walked through Main Street, which was pretty quiet with the First Generation gone even with the five newcomers. Jack was in the bay, three people were on the beach, Adimen and Artea were in the fields, there were a couple more people in the fields and at the barn, Tina was in the silo or cleaning somewhere, Victor attended to the bathroom, Perry and the twins were in the kitchen, and others were here and there doing what was needed. By her count there must have been another seven people; she had a few faces in mind but could not put names to them. Meeting new people was not something she had ever done until about a week ago but once she'd met them all, she wouldn't have anyone else to meet, except maybe on Robin, but they were a bit peculiar and it didn't seem like they were going to return there anytime soon. She walked past the forum where it was really loud. Perry could be heard laughing and she could picture the twins throwing food across the kitchen, which she, of course, disapproved of but still, it made her smile. Looking back, she then realized that even though she always liked the twins, she had never got close to them. Her friendship with Tom was always much stronger and it would probably remain this way, but she had developed a real soft spot for them this past week. They had proven to be great people, even in adversity, and was this not what defined great people? She realized she had stopped walking and was lost in her thoughts and smelling the delicious food coming from the kitchen. She looked around for a while feeling a bit stupid to just be standing there and wondered if anyone had seen her. Then, she told herself that after fishing each morning for two hours, it would be difficult to work another two in a kitchen without eating anything. She turned right towards the entrance of the bathroom when a boy rushed out from the right side.

"Clean towels coming through!" he said enthusiastically.

She had noticed him the night before philosophizing with Tina. His attire was more colorful than anyone else and he seemed to be the only one who was able to have a conversation up to Tina's standards. Artea was Tina's friend, but he did not speak like her, it was just one of those friendships where they were so different that it worked.

"Here, take a towel, get some clothes from the bathroom and tell your friends where they are. I stored your old clothes as they were really dirty. Sweaty, sweaty!" He went on singing and rushed past her into the bathroom.

She walked into the empty lobby and saw him go into the shower room, singing and dancing as he walked over to the shelves where all the towels were professionally folded.

She took off her underwear and decided to go into one of the private showers. The Robartians would really think she was lazy if she spent a lot of time on her own but she needed time to herself. She started wondering what her dad and her mom were doing at this moment. Were they dead? Were they on the mountain somewhere? Maybe in trouble? Had they just vanished? She wondered if they missed her or if they were happy, as happy as she was because she felt weirdly happy. She missed some of her old life, mostly her parents and Maggie. Then, when she thought of her, a new feeling grew in her, that they must have died and it was oddly reassuring as it meant she was not abandoned but something had happened to them against their will. Of course, she trusted her parents more, but for some reason, she knew Maggie's betrayal would be impossible as she was the one person she trusted.

A good 25 minutes later, she finally stepped out of the water. Her skin was dry from spending so much time in the ocean and in the shower. She walked to one of the benches and found a few bags there. One of them had her

name on it and said, 'For Indarra, return what doesn't fit.'
Each bag was named and had the same note. She threw
her dirty underwear in the hamper, opened the bag, and
put on the first thing she found. It was a sleeveless, strap-
less blue dress with a rope like a belt. It was simple but
efficient and weirdly monochrome for the village. She put
on her black flip-flops and carried the bag back to her
room. She was going to open the bag and look through it
and start trying everything on and then unpack it all into
her closet, but if she did she would end up being even too
late for lunch so she threw the bag on the bench at the
front of her bed and walked straight outside. Well, first
she glimpsed at herself in the mirror at the corner of the
room and really liked what she saw; she looked young,
simple, confident, and her hair was a harmonious messy
wave. She was ready to do something new.

When she walked into the kitchen in the forum, it was
almost 11 AM and it was a lot quieter than when she had
walked by the building 40 minutes earlier. The twins were
on the floor behind one of the counters cleaning what
looked like the entire contents of an oversized Dutch oven.

"Oh, you're here," said Ross looking a little flushed.
"So, we lost our balance."

"We? Are you like one person in two bodies? How
can you both lose your balance?" asked Indarra a little
annoyed this time.

"Well, we were sure we could both hold one side of the Dutch oven and swing it while keeping all the liquid in there; you know, centrifugal force! Tom's mom taught us that!" said Ross almost proudly, as if remembering what centrifugal force was could make up for the mess.

"And it worked!" continued Turk. "It all stayed in, as long as we were swinging it that is," and he looked at his brother smirking. "But then we swung it a little harder and it got really heavy, so much that when it bounced back on the other side we couldn't control it anymore and it dragged the both of us against that wall and the whole thing fell on the ground . . ."

"In our defense, nobody taught us about the force that keeps things to the ground," laughed Ross.

"Alright, I'm gonna ignore all this, Perry, I'm truly sorry, for them and for being late; my double shift will need a few adjustments. How about I show how much I deserve this job by taking charge this morning?" asked Indarra while slicing up a couple of veggies.

"No problem, go ahead. It's an hour and a half before lunch and we need to start everything over so . . . good luck!" Perry did not seem annoyed but actually amused by the twins. He had a brother so he probably enjoyed the lively atmosphere he'd had in his kitchen since their arrival, as messy as it got.

"Alright, one of you!" she pointed at the twins. "There's a 45 kg tuna sitting on the peer on the left side of the bay. Tell Jack that Indarra said it was OK to take it as we need it for lunch. Your foolishness will not amuse him so try to be convincing enough without telling him about your little centrifugal experiment. The other twin," she continued bossily still pointing at them but at none of them in particular, "can finish cleaning here and start slicing up onions and garlic. Perry, would you like to go see Adimen and Artea with me so we can get what we need?"

He nodded. They all stepped out of the kitchen, except for Turk who was busy scrubbing the floors. Indarra and Perry went left up Main Street and made it to the fields where Adimen was holding a notepad, pointing at different things, and speaking really fast. Artea seemed interested in everything else around him from the clouds to a fly buzzing around him but not to Adimen's comments, so much so that he noticed Indarra and Perry the second they walked out of the forum.

"Hey guys, how is everything going here?" asked Indarra giving Artea a sorry look.

"Really well, agriculture is fascinating, it really is, but we could really improve production," said Adimen. "See here, they grew tomatoes and then cabbage but because of the length of their roots, it would have been better to use broccoli to give the soil a rest for a couple of seasons. Then, for diversity, if we installed bridges here and—"

"Wow, this is fascinating. I'm glad you guys are making such a fantastic team," interrupted Indarra ignoring Adimen's angry look. "Listen, there has been a little err . . ."

"The twins?" asked Adimen.

"Yes, we need veggies and starch, for lunch," said Indarra looking at Perry. "I think that's what they dropped."

"Yes, dinner has been cooked, ready to be quickly reheated tonight."

"Maybe a quick puree of broccoli, sweet potato, and butternut? If you have some sage it would be great too," commanded Indarra.

"No problem, let me wrap this up for you. I'll go get it from the silo," said Artea and he walked away quickly.

"It's a good thing I got here; the growing system was really archaic and wait till I stick my nose in the barn!" said Adimen feeling important.

"Oh, I'm sure they can't wait!" said Indarra sarcastically but Adimen didn't seem to notice.

A few minutes later, Artea called to them from the silo. He had three large trays full of vegetables. They all took one and Artea helped them carry the boxes all the way to the kitchen. They bumped into Ross, struggling on his way up with the enormous sea monster.

"And you thought you won by being the one who did not have to clean," laughed Turk when he saw his brother coming in.

Ross was covered in fish blood and other gooey things.

"We have an hour and a half. Since the meat stew is gone," said Indarra looking at the twins a little amused now, "it's going to be tuna sashimi and veggie purée. Ross, you already reek of fish so you will have an hour and . . ." she looked at the clock on the wall, "10 minutes to turn this whole tuna into sashimi. Turk, have you already sliced the garlic and onions?" He nodded. "Good, get the Dutch oven, olive oil, sage onions, garlic, and put it all in! Meanwhile, start peeling all the vegetables. I will help you for about 20 minutes with Perry and then you are on your own. You boil them all but keep the broth and don't put in too much water at a time as we will not make it like a traditional puree, I want it thicker. As it won't have time to be cooked on time in pieces, start blending it with a stick blender early on. Don't forget salt, pepper, and milk at the end but make sure it doesn't burn and that it stays thick. It can't fill the whole plate and drawn the sashimi alright? It needs to be more like a paste!"

Indarra was really proud of herself. She had managed to do more than what she was expected to in both her jobs in basically half the time that she was given and she knew they all knew it, even Jack. By now, a good quarter of the tuna had turned into delicious boneless slices of raw fish. All the sweet potatoes had been cut and diced while a good half of the butternut squashes had been seeded and Turk was going to be on his own to take care of the other half and trim the broccoli. Under Indarra's instructions and Perry's approving eye, she added the stalks. They had to be peeled, diced, and added to the recipe, which gave Turk a lot more work but he understood that it was not up for discussion and above all, it was not time to argue after the Dutch oven catastrophe. Once all of this done, all he had to do was turn it into something edible to save the day.

"So, this is how we do things," started Perry, tiptoeing a little and trying not to sound too bossy. "But of course nothing's set in stone. As you know, our afternoon activities are really important to us, so we try to keep our schedules clear for it as much as we can. The only person here who is on duty 24 hours a day is my brother, though he will only work mornings for benign pathologies, routine appointments, and to give medication. Of course, if you fall off a tree at three in the afternoon and break your leg, he won't tell you that he is busy finger-painting and that you should wait till the morning after, but you get the point. Here in the forum, it's the same, but we can minimize our work in the afternoons to a few minutes a day. Remember that here, everyone has his or her job, and we don't ask anyone to go and clean their own dishes. It's a waste of time and each task is done faster if accomplished by one or a limited group of people.

"We might like philosophy and our crafts," he said with a smile, as he probably knew that the newcomers might have found their obsession with painting slightly ridiculous or at least unusual, "but we believe in efficiency and we want our afternoons off. So, we arrive in the morning, like everyone else around 7.30 AM, have our breakfast, go shower, and get ready We start at 8.30 AM. The first thing we used to do was take the garbage to the round-house, but we don't know how to get in so we're accumulating it behind the forum for now and thinking of burning it. Then we do the dishes that accumulated in this room from lunch and dinner yesterday, and breakfast this morning. It's pretty easy with both dishwashers, but it's still a one-man job for an hour and a half so we take turns to do that. I'll create a schedule for all of us so we know what to do and when. You'll always be with Jack when we wash up so luckily you won't ever have to do it," said Perry looking at Indarra. "Then we make the menu for the next three meals for the day after. Considering we'll be making menus together but that you are fishing when I used to do it, from now on, we will make the menus two days ahead in the morning."

"I could just design the menu first and then go fishing, but the fish do start to hide when the sun is too high," explained Indarra, before realizing this was silly.

"It would be complicated for you. You would have to rush to shower after fishing as Jack does. It's a bit messy and this is really no bother this way, we just need to adapt a little. Back to it!" said Perry with determination. "Usually, one of the cooks would give the people at the farm the ingredients list around 9:30 AM so they have time to prepare everything by 12 to bring it over at lunchtime so we can cook it the day after. The other cook, well, there are now two of you, starts preparing breakfast and dinner. Breakfast is fruit, cereals, and some sort of protein by itself or in bread if there are no cereals on the side. We put everything in a brown bag on that shelf back here in the pantry. Dinner has to be something they can help themselves to like a soup or something with a broth but sometimes we do cottage pies or lasagna if we feel like it. However, it will dry out or get cold if one of us is not around really taking care of it. Salads work pretty well too. If it's a cold dish we just lay a huge bowl of it on the counter with all the cutlery needed. We also have to prepare dessert, be it a cake or just fruit. Then comes lunch. This is the meal we prepare with more care because we serve it and we can cook it last minute if we want to as we work a little later than everyone else. It's not much, but technically we work 10 minutes more than the last person served. So, then we set up everything for lunch, cutlery, plates, glasses and we always make three courses. The first comers arrive around 12:20 PM and those are usually people working in food like Jack, Artea, and the butchers . . . They bring us what we need for the next day. From now on, this will be when we will give them the list of everything we need for them to bring the day after.

"Once the last person is served, we serve ourselves and eat. Once people are done, including us, they put their dirty dishes on the shelf next to the counter. At the end of the afternoon, once everyone has relaxed from their day, we all head to the Forum for dinner. One of us will take a turn to arrive 10 minutes early to reheat the pot if it's a stew and take out whatever is needed for dinner. And if it's not hot, they bitch!" Perry giggled a little and switched right back to business. "Anyway, at 7:30 PM, turn the gas to a minimum so it keeps it warm. The last person to help him or herself turns the gas off; they will know they're the last coz they have picked up the last plate." Perry stopped for a few seconds and looked around, wondering what he had to explain next. "After dinner, it's the same thing again; dirty dishes go on the same shelf. Oh, I forgot, the person who reheats dinner also pulls out the table with tomorrow's breakfast on it and makes sure there are coffee beans in the coffee machine and there you have it. It's simple and we start all over again the day after." He finished looking highly satisfied!

"Alright, well, that was incredibly detailed, very logical, and everything seems to make sense. So if I paid attention properly, I would say that it's time to make the menu for tomorrow and the day after since we need to catch up?" said Indarra trying to seem like a good student.

"No, I already made the menu for tomorrow so the food will be brought today for tomorrow but we do need to prepare a list today to give it to the food people at lunch for them to bring the food tomorrow at lunch for the day after. So what are we having in two days?" he asked looking at Indarra all excited.

"Well, I was thinking maybe a minced beef coconut curry with mushrooms. Did you know that a whole bunch of mushrooms is actually one living entity? So, that could be for dinner, with quinoa. We'll need lemongrass lemon . . ." she stopped and added, "I'll write down the list and maybe pomegranate for dessert, one half each?"

Perry made a face and said, "We're maintaining pomegranates in the village to keep the breed going of course, but we're not overproducing them as most of the fruit goes to waste you see . . ."

"Should we have basil strawberries for dessert?" asked Indarra tentatively while the twins looked at each other not understanding what the deal was with the pomegranates.

"Sure, shouldn't small things like herbs be against your beliefs?" asked Perry trying to tease her in a friendly way but somehow he started blushing and made it all a little awkward.

"I try to make a difference if it's something that's part of a group and can be regrown. I don't believe the shoot is the creature; in my opinion, it's the whole plant so cutting it actually makes it healthier!"

"Alright, and for lunch—" Perry began before Indarra interrupted him.

"Well, in case you don't have an idea yet, I did think of something for lunch. We should finish whatever Jack has caught. These small fish, defenseless . . ." she added looked out of the window for dramatic effect. "We could make filets out of all of them and maybe grill some peppers and cabbage, then we could tell Jack to stop fishing minuscule fishes but instead only fish one a day, but a big one. I could get a swordfish for the day after that." She looked at Perry for a bit, hesitating about saying what she really wanted to, but after a few seconds, she decided she'd say it even if it was not pleasant. "Honestly, I don't even need Jack, I can get one each day myself that would feed the whole village for a whole meal, just saying."

"I hear your point," said Perry embarrassed, "and I agree that it is great if you can get a fish that feeds all of us every day. But everyone has a job here and it is nobody's job to put someone out of a job or change it. He's not bothering anyone. I mean, if one day we're short in the production of meat or fruit or any job, then we can create jobs, but here, if something, we just have too much fish, so it's not considered an issue. How about, each time you catch more than 30 kg of fish, then the day after you don't have to go fish so that we don't end up having too much of it and waste it? Or you can go and just swim; nobody would blame you when you're already bringing in so much!"

"It's not ideal, but I'll find a way to let him know somehow that it's pointless to get this many little fish. Alright, for now, let's say that we're set. I'll get octopus or squid if we have enough fish and we'll make nice starters with them! See, I can be flexible," she smiled and started opening drawers here and there.

"Good then, Alright, it's now 12:10 PM and people will arrive soon. Let's get organized. For the starter, we have cold lotus root lasagna with radish top pesto. It's healthy and delicious," he said smiling sounding like he was straight out of one of those commercials where they tell you not to eat too much sugar, fat, and salt. "Make sure every single one of them is set on the counter for people to help themselves. We have trays, cutlery, and glasses. Ross, take the plates away, it's not dinner, we're serving them their main course, thaaaank you," Perry said in a sing-song voice. "They will get a tray from here. Get the lasagna, yes it's a starter, then they will walk to Ross. Indarra, you can stand by the starter in case they have questions and because there are four of us and I don't know what to do with all of us. Ross, you take a plate, stack it with 12 pieces of sashimi, I'll sprinkle the sesame seeds on top and fill small cups of soy sauce and add wasabi to the plate, then I'll hand the plate to Turk who will make a nice dome shaped puree. Nice dome shape, alright?"

Turk nodded unconvinced.

"So, I just get to stand here like an idiot?" asked Indarra feeling left out.

"I don't know. Maybe you can just go sit and eat or . . ." he looked at Indarra's angry face and added, "OK, what about you take my position and I'll prepare four trays for us, does that sound good?"

"See, compromising!" said Indarra amused.

The twins had been very quiet since their Dutch oven event and that was really unlike them. The first people to show up were Tatiana and Roger from the barn. Roger was a skinny, short, pale man and his eyes were so clear they were almost see-through. Tatiana had really curly hair and no actual haircut. She was also short but very muscular.

"Hello there, got your order, Perry," Tatiana said. She seemed to be the only one in this place to have a different accent from the others. "Look at what we got here; that's one nice lamb rack, huh? Don't go mess it up, buddy! We don't want it all dry again this time!"

"Hmm, OK, thanks," said Perry. He seemed a bit taken aback by this comment.

"And here are two kilos of lard." She dumped it heavily on the counter.

Perry looked at it with slight disgust, picked it up, and asked them to start getting their food while marching to the fridge with the bags of meat. Indarra handed Tatiana the list of products that they needed to bring tomorrow at lunchtime.

"What's that green mess in my wheel-shaped potato, huh? Is that even cooked?" Tatiana asked.

Perry spent a lot of time with his head in the fridge arranging and rearranging the food even though the fridge was half-empty. The two butchers finally made their way up to the terrace with another comment about people being so lazy they couldn't even cook their fish.

A minute later, Jack arrived with a full basket of fish, sea-bass, shrimps, and mussels. Indarra tried not to look and wondered what dish they could make out of all these different fish, but the transaction altogether was much quieter than the last. Once again, Perry walked to the fridge with the basket of fish. Jack helped himself without much comment aside from a quiet thank you and walked off with his food after getting his list.

At 12:24 PM, Adimen entered, followed immediately by Artea.

"Alright, this is the first round; we have tomatoes, garlic, fennel leaves, thyme, bay leaves, and oranges. We'll come back with a fruit basket and with the pumpkins," said Artea, out of breath and sweaty, followed by a really flushed Adimen.

After that, everyone else started to arrive more or less together. Tom was last with Tina and Louis. They had probably gone to shower after their work out. Once everyone was served, the four chefs went up to the terrace with their trays. Seating was always awkward now there was so few of them as you did not want to form smaller groups or intrude on other's friendships either. Tom and Tina sat with Artea and Adimen. Jack was a friend of Artea's so he sat there too. Also, Louis decided to join them as they had just worked out together and he was a friend of Tina's. Then, of course, the four cooks joined them, so the terrace turned into one huge table and two smaller ones. Weirdly, Victor sat at the barn people's table. Indarra didn't see what they could possibly have in common aside from the fact that their workplaces were geographically close!

"So, did everyone have a good day at work?" asked Artea without really asking anyone in particular, and then added, "a good first day?"

"Yes, it was fascinating!" said Adimen. "There is still so much work ahead to perfect our system but this is all so challenging. Although, from a scientific point of view, if we actually perfected it it would be almost pointless as we would produce way too much food unless we start maybe exchanging with the other villages."

This would be the sentence that made R.O.B enter the trading era.

"That's actually not a stupid idea," said Indarra without noticing Adimen's face who did not appreciate the word stupid in a sentence that concerned her. "I mean this is something we would have to really plan ahead for once we've figured out what we're gonna do about the information we get from our travels. We would have to find an easy way to take it from one village to the other; that's a very difficult task."

However, The one thing Indarra did not say is that she was a little surprised that Adimen had mentioned trading with other villages when the day before she had said she did not want to tell those they had left behind that they had found other villages.

"Anyway, this is just an idea as it's true we don't know how we are going to deal with the other villages," added Adimen as if her commonsense had suddenly taken over her will to do her job perfectly. "So, how was your first day, guys?"

All three of them started mumbling something and complaining quietly about their own little problems. However, in the end, they were actually all pretty happy about their mornings, even the twins!

"I'm a jock here!" joked Tom. "I have the biggest arms of all the Robartians, except Artea's . . . Why are yours so big by the way? You grew up painting! That's not fair! Anyway, I liked it. No competition, just relaxing, stretching, a little cardio, a few pushups, and they're already dying. You guys can carve my name on the door of my bungalow, I'm staying!"

Everyone laughed. Tina, who was clearly not in great shape, said how much she had suffered and probably would not be able to raise her arms higher than shoulder level for the next month . . . When lunch ended, everyone took their trays back downstairs and walked to the beach.

"So, we thought today we would not work on movie making but show you all the other activities. When you met us yesterday, we were all doing our own things on the beach. That's what we'll be doing with you today so you'll get to try a bit of everything and tonight we will have an exhibition of our work. Tomorrow night, Victor and Tina will introduce us to the new project."

"Why Victor and Tina?" asked Tom.

"Well, Victor is the movie director and Tina is the scenarist who writes the stories, so they get to present their project to us. It's always a little stressful because, well, Tina is part of it and sometimes the crowd doesn't agree and wants to shoot a different kind of movie. I love being a stunt in the movies, that's what I'm good at, but to be honest, I don't know all the things they do. I've always been sort of an outsider of all this. Of course, I can teach you some, but you will do much better learning from the rest of the crowd. Alright, let's get you all settled with someone. Turk, you can go with Tatiana."

Raw panic appeared in Turk's eyes, Tatiana being the mad butcher. Apparently, she was great at sculpting.

"So, are you the one who did not cook my fish or the one who mashed grass into my starter?" asked Tatiana as if she was about to smash a statue on Turk's head.

"Actually neither!" said Ross feeling a little better. "I made the veggie mash thing!"

"Really? Where did my meat go?" Tatiana asked.

"What? What meat?" Turk looked left and right for help but everyone was busy.

"The meat I gave Perry the day before. Eight kilos of beef. Where did that go?"

"I err . . ." he hesitated a second, "I dropped the Dutch oven on the floor," and he added hurriedly, "with my brother!"

"Well, it probably is a good thing as he always over-cooks my meat!"

For a second Turk felt like maybe he could be in team Tatiana, whatever that was . . .

"You sculpted before?" she asked casually as if making people pee their pants were part of her daily activities and she was not at all concerned about what had just happened.

"Nope." Turk stuck his fingers in the grey mass before him and Tatiana slapped his hand.

"Today we're using clay; you mix it with water and then start giving it a shape. How about you make me a nice big gut receptacle!"

"Hmm, a what?" Turk swallowed his saliva and looked for a familiar face once again but everyone was still very focused on what they were doing.

"For my guts, when I gut stuff." Tatiana pretended to stretch Turk's abdomen and pulled from one hand, she wasn't trying to scare him, she simply was surprised he hadn't understood the word gut and had figured miming would help. "I dropped a ribcage on my last one so it broke . . ." Tatiana started showing him how to mold the clay while she worked on her woodwork, forming it into an ugly figurine with a knife and a hammer. "Come on, little girl. Stick your fingers in there already. Don't just tap around it, give it a proper shape. I want this thing to be able to contain at least a whole cow's guts or," she added smirking, "a pair of twins."

Turk wondered if maybe she wasn't as crazy as everyone thought, but instead, she was just playing tough.

Not far from there, Ross was on brewing duty with Tina. This was not exactly an official craft in Robart but she had really insisted she wanted to teach him and said she saw a brewer in him. Closer to the water, Artea was teaching Tom how to make glass with sand and how they made actual glasses for the forum.

"See, I don't get the point of all the rest of the stuff they do," explained Artea. "Well, pottery maybe as we need it for the forum too and it has a real purpose, but some of those things I'm like, what is it for?"

Tom looked at Adimen who sat alone a bit further away, making plates; they were just like the ones they had in their own forums.

"Wait a minute, you make plates here too? The plates you eat from at the forum?" asked Tom suspiciously.

"Yes, we do," replied Artea.

"So you mean you copy them from the ones made in the roundhouse?"

"Hmm, no, the roundhouse doesn't make them; they're all made by us! They're always plain grey with—"

"Different drawings at the top of the plates," Tom interrupted.

"Yeah," replied Artea with his beautiful uncomprehending smile.

"And you're sure the roundhouse does not make them? Wait, would it even make a difference?" he said as if thinking aloud. "Adimen, do you see what you're doing? You're making our plates!"

"I know, it's exciting!" she said, all business-like.

"No, I mean, those are our plates, back in our village, plates which only they make, which have ended up in our villages. Indarra, come to see this!"

Indarra walked over to Tom and Adimen.

"Oh, that's cute, Adimen, good job." It could have sounded patronizing but somehow it didn't. "I did not pay attention, but they really do look like ours," said Indarra.

"Because they are ours, Indarra!" said Tom over articulating each syllable. "We've been eating off plates made by Robartians in Robat, and so have they in Robin. How is that possible?"

"I don't know, could it just be a coincidence? I mean, a plate is a plate, they look similar, but it does not mean it's theirs. Maybe back where we're from it's not a craft so it comes out of the roundhouse like all the rest." She looked away for a moment as if she needed to think more about it, and then she finally said, "OK it's weird."

Tom started looking through the pile of plates. "OK there it is!" he said triumphantly. "Remember those funny plates with the toothbrush on it? We never understood why they would put a toothbrush on a plate and you thought it was to remind us to brush our teeth after lunch. Well, somehow they want them to remember this here too!" he said sarcastically. "And it's a paintbrush, not a toothbrush! That's why it ended up on the plates."

"Oh, these are mine!" interrupted Louis excitedly, "I like drawing paintbrushes with a paintbrush; it's like painting into a mirror!"

Adimen rolled her eyes and Artea just looked away.

"Well, on the upside, we might be able to start swapping merchandise more easily than we thought, Adimen," said Indarra with a hint of annoyance in her voice.

Adimen suddenly became interested in glass making. She seemed fascinated by how the sand turned into glass, that is until she realized the glasses were also exactly like the ones they had back in Robin so she decided to quickly move on to something else. Then she stepped back and looked at everyone and all they were doing. How could she not have seen it?

Her little diversion was enough for people to stop thinking about it, oddly, it did not seem to appear as such a shock for the Robartians. For the newcomers though, it was a different thing. They all looked at each other and understood immediately that it was probably not something to be discussed publicly. Adimen then hurried to the brewing station where Indarra was also working now.

"Oh, wow, Tina! That looks like so much fun; please tell me everything about it. I wanna know it all. Take your time!" lied Adimen.

And learn everything she did! After some time, she started liking it as it was a fun process. It was a little frustrating as it took a long time but was still fun. Everyone went about their business for a while and then retired to their rooms or the bathroom to freshen up from the long day before dinner. Dinner was rather uneventful. It was Indarra's turn to warm the food up 10 minutes ahead. People sat at five tables instead of three this time. The four newcomers sat at one table with Artea and Tina, just like at their first meal here. They wanted to discuss the plate and glass issue but it was too risky to talk about in front of everyone. So, everyone went on joking about this and that and talked about their day. Tina convinced Indarra to try a few of her potions as she really deserved it having worked so hard on it all day. This annoyed Adimen as she had worked even harder. She did not want to drink, but she wanted her efforts, even fake, to be recognized. By the third potion, Indarra developed a taste for it and had a few more. Saying she was tipsy was an understatement.

"So, Adimen!" started Artea, "I could not help but notice how you suddenly changed topics earlier on the beach, why is that?"

"Listen, Artea, I don't know. This is all so weird for us. We've been here for 24 hours now and come from villages you didn't know existed. Our parents all vanished overnight and we found out the mountain is not dangerous and we've been lied to all our lives. However, so far we thought we had only been lied to within our respective villages, but maybe that's not the case either. There could be an explanation for all this and perhaps our parents were unaware of it." Adimen looked down for a moment as if she was processing the information as she explained it. "However, if the villages were exchanging goods, somebody had to know, they had to know. It makes it all so real to all of us, you know, the betrayal. It makes it all so real for you. I did not think your people needed a reminder of this."

"Unless," started Indarra, "what if there was no betrayal. Maybe they were not telling us for our own good. What if this was all random or maybe there was betrayal but just from a few people, like those working at the roundhouse. Nobody knew what they were doing in there, as it's always been so secretive. So maybe only they knew and maybe that was no betrayal either. They could have had a good reason not to tell us or maybe informing us was going to take part during the transition. Perhaps our original training was supposed to be within our own villages and then we would start communicating with the other villages. Why? I don't know why!" she was saying as if she was answering to a question someone had asked her. "But we just don't know so far and yes I agree with you Adimen that there is no point bringing it up too much in front of everyone. The only thing it will do is confuse people and make them feel like crap."

"Indarra, by thinking like this," started Ross, "you are no better than our parents who probably lied to us our whole life. You say it was done to protect people but maybe it's because that's just convenient for you to believe. If we don't worry about it, we can completely forget about the other two villages and just stay here happily."

"Ross, you're being unfair. I don't think I've been selfish. There's no perfect way of doing this and nobody told us how to act when this situation would come along. I'm doing what seems right here, but if you have a better idea, please take charge. I have not seen you do much of that today," said Indarra looking away. She wanted to say more but somehow didn't feel good about it and couldn't actually make eye contact with him or she'd lose her confidence.

Ross got up and left with only half of his food eaten which would have upset Indarra on any other occasion but she did not notice it this time.

"Alrighty, fun things are about to commence!" announced Tina theatrically. "Let's set up the exhibition, yeah!" she said as if she had not noticed what had just happened. With one glass of pear liquor in hand, she stumbled out of her seat almost hitting Jerry in the head with her tray.

Everyone started walking toward the beach. They got torches from the closet behind the school and stuck them in the sand. It looked beautiful with the calm sea of the lagoon behind them. Everyone set their work on the sand or on tables. Tina had arranged all her bottles by color. Some were clear and others were a bright red – maybe a strawberry liquor? Louis had displayed paintings on trees where you could see large paintbrushes on different colored backgrounds. James had made sculptures that were really realistic wood or clay structures of houses and mountains. Also, there was an incredible flat board, which represented the sea, and it seemed like he had melted something on top of it that resembled the ocean and almost seemed to move. It was probably related to skills he'd acquired in his afternoon job as a movie set designer. Indarra walked from one station to the next, trying to focus on them instead of thinking of what had happened with Ross during dinner. She decided to leave the exhibition for a bit, passing by the dance station where Phil was performing with Victor while Jerry was playing some kind of instrument. Last, she passed by Tina's station.

"You know, he really likes you!" said Tina

"What?" asked Indarra, surprised by how normal Tina's voice suddenly sounded.

"Otherwise, he would have been mad at your friend Adimen too!" Tina giggled and went back to her activities.

Indarra sat on a log on the beach by the school. It was easy to be alone around there since no one used this building anymore. She started thinking about her friend-ships and how Tom had always been a part of her life. The twins had never been as close but they both had a special place in her heart and she had grown closer to them this past week. Then she started thinking of Tom's mom whom she missed so much. Of course, she missed her own parents but she really wished Maggie was around now as she would know what to do and how to deal with the situation. Unless she too was a traitor and had faked being nice to her her whole life. She mumbled out her thoughts as she tapped frenetically on the log she was sitting on.

"It's not my brother, it's just a log, stop woman handling it!" interrupted Turk

"Crap, sorry, I guess I was kinda lost in my thoughts. You're not having fun at the exhibition?" asked Indarra.

"Yeah . . . it was fun for a while, then I got bored. The dancing was fun though. That's the only common activity that we have with them, did you notice?"

"Oh, you're right, I did not think about that."

"Looking forward to stunt training tomorrow?" asked Turk casually, not daring to bring up Ross.

"Please girl, I was born to do that. I'll be the one training Artea, not the other way around, even though he is twice my size. Actually, it will be to my advantage because if I have to fall from the roof of a burning house, I'll fall more lightly whereas he'll crash like a tree," she said changing her expression slightly as if she was actually just realizing now what the job would be like.

"I don't know if they would actually make you drop from the roof of a house. Don't they have props for this or something? On the other hand, when it starts raining tables and they smash on you, you're just bones and they'll break you!" And they both started laughing. "Alright, I think they are about to pack everything up and go to bed.

196

You gonna be OK?" asked Turk, giving her a friendly slap on the leg.

"Sure, I'll just be here another minute. You have a good night and I'll see you tomorrow OK?"

"Alright, good night, you take care."

"Good night, Turk!"

Turk got up and headed to his bungalow and Indarra got up a couple minutes later.

"Who is that?" asked Ross when he heard a knock.

"It's me," answered Indarra the way you'd do to a parent expecting your visit.

"Oh, OK, I'm coming." He put on a shirt quickly and opened the door. "Sorry, I did not want you to admire my beautiful body so I had to put my clothes back on," he said in what seemed his jokey usual way but Indarra knew he was just pretending because he was feeling uncomfortable.

"I just wanted to say that I was sorry."

"What are you sorry about? I'm the one who freaked out out of nowhere, I'm not even sure why I got mad so I can't even imagine your confusion."

"Well, I was not sure, but that's not something you would usually do so, I don't know, I figured that you must have had a good reason."

"Wow, that's really sweet of you. Pushover!" he said with a smirk.

"Says the little baby hiding in his bungalow."

"Hey, don't make this too real! Let's not mention this again!" He blushed a little and pretended to fold something so he could turn his back on Indarra.

"I promise, my sweet boy!" she said in a dramatic pretend posh voice and opened her arms very theatrically, spun around, and headed towards her bungalow.

Chapter 8

FLOATING ON AIR!

Everyone was laughing, smiling, and cracking jokes. Everyone's mood was at its best and nothing could ruin the evening. Indarra had had a few more drinks than planned and was one sip away from taking her top off to celebrate, even though the night was extremely cold. Everyone was walking joyfully. Some held hands, some were kissing, and others were just plain happy and did not need to show it in any way as their simple sense of bliss was all they needed.

"Are you ready for two hours of otic orgasms?" I asked.

"OK and now you are going to tell us again that you're not obsessed?" said Artea.

The night was cold but beautiful. The group enjoyed the smells of the night, its noises, and its colors. Artea looked more *handsome than ever. It was impossible for people not to look at him and what was even more incredible was that he was unaware of it. This was a perfect cocktail for his absolute raw sexuality. Indarra had once told him he was so hot he had looped out of most people's sexual spectrum and no longer registered as a sexual entity and she was probably right. His smile, beauty, and kindness just hypnotized people wherever he went. This is why, a few minutes later, the nervous man still managed to smile back at him, even if it was a very timid smile. His face almost looked deformed and the blood was beating so hard in his temples he could barely hear how loud it was around him. Maybe it was the fear or the excitement or whatever chemical unbalance was getting the best of his body, so much that he dropped the object from under his jacket and it fell at Artea's feet. The man froze completely and Artea could see the veins in his eyes. What Artea interpreted as sadness made him want to help the man so he picked up the object and handed it back to the uncomprehending man while giving him an Artea smile that included not only his mouth but also his eyes and entire face. That's when a timid smile appeared on the man's face. However, it was so sweaty it was hard to tell if there were tears of sadness there or ones of longing.*

Indarra woke up to the sounds of Robart stirring outside her thin bungalow walls. She had also slept with her windows open. She got up, put on a shirt, shorts, and flip-flops, and walked out of her bungalow. She saw Turk coming out of Ross' bungalow with Ross, which she thought was a bit odd but would explain why they were so synchronized. She caught up with them at the entrance of the forum and they all grabbed their breakfast bag, a cup of coffee, and walked up to the terrace. Most people were already there. They sat with Artea, Tina, Adimen, and Tom who were already half-way through their breakfast.

"So, today is going to be a big day for you guys. You're going to take your first steps in cinema and you're gonna love it. It's so much fun. Are you guys excited?" asked Artea, almost hysterical.

"I'm just scared I'm going to be too good an actor and you guys are going to send me back to Robat out of fear that I'm going to shine too bright and make you all feel ridiculous in the process!" said Turk quickly as if it had been rehearsed.

"Speaking of which," started Indarra, "I think we owe it to the rest of the villages to tell them what's going on. It's not fair that we all get to live happily here while they are left behind."

"What difference does it make? We're not living differently knowing that there are three villages instead of one," said Tom.

"Tom, I'm sure you know it's the right thing. We have to go back, at least for a day, maybe two. We can leave really early and split up. A small group can go to Robat and the other to Robin. We will tell them what we know and let them do whatever they want. Whether they decide to stay or feel like traveling for the day or maybe come for the night, we could have a bungalow for visitors where we host them. They could come and discover the habits, the food, the architecture, the difference in sunsets, and all the other little things that make each place unique. Maybe we could start swapping products as we said before and if some of them want to move then they'll just move. There's room for more people here for sure and they have room there for people from here who maybe will decide to go as well. I know it's a little ideological, we will encounter some problems, and we clearly have a good thing going here, but we have to do it."

"To be honest," started Turk, "everyone here knows that there are another two villages and no one has gone so far. What makes you think they would?"

"Well, I hope they will, even the Robartians. They're more than free to head there right now and introduce themselves as we did only 36 hours ago to Artea. Yes, it has only been 36 hours," said Indarra reminding Turk that people clearly hadn't had time to organize anything to go and explore the other villages. "People are still digesting the fact that they have met new people for the first time in their lives. It's not going to take much longer before they get over that and decide they wanna see more. Curiosity will make them want to do that. Adimen, you're really good at planning and I think we would all benefit by listening to you about organization but I thought we could maybe go as two groups of maybe four or five people. Perhaps half should be from here so they know we're speaking the truth."

"That sounds really good," said Adimen. "I agree, maybe two of you guys should go to Robat and take another two from here. I think that's enough as we don't want too large a group to overwhelm them. I should obviously be in the Robin team as they'll need to see one of theirs, along with two of you guys and another Robartian. OK, let's think, Indarra, I think you need to lead your group back to your village and we have to separate the twins because I can't bring this news with something as odd as twins. Sorry, guys, they've just never met twins where I am from even though we know they exist. So, the Robat team will be Indarra, Ross, Perry, and Artea. Then in my group will be Turk, Tom, and Phil? Phil and Perry would say yes, right?"

"I'm sure they would," said Artea. "Let me ask them. Phil, Perry, come over here!" He waved for them to come over from the other table.

"Hey, guys!" said an overly smiling Phil. "Oh, Adimen, we're going to be such great partners!" he said while slapping Adimen in the back who almost burned herself with her cup of coffee. "Ready for your big start? We're about to create magic, girl! So, what are we talking about?"

They filled them in about their little project and both Phil and Perry agreed to join the mission. Phil was really excited and could not wait to make it into a movie and 'CGI the crap out of it' as he would say.

"Oh, one condition though," added Perry, "that tonight we tell the village about our plan. They deserve to know what's going on."

Not everyone seemed to agree, including Adimen, but somehow, in the end, everyone did or at least did not protest too much.

"I'll organize our bags tonight. We'll take one bag with a bit of water in it and some fruit that we'll pass around. We don't need more as we can have lunch when we arrive at the other village. Of course, unless it takes longer and we spend a night over but let's not worry everyone by doing that."

"Should we tell them about the plates?" asked Turk cautiously.

"What plates?" asked Phil.

"Now that he is in we might as well tell him," said Indarra.

Once they explained everything, Phil seemed surprised but also more exhilarated by the idea. Once the conversation settled and breakfast was eaten, everyone headed off to their morning jobs

"Hey! Tom! So, you are going to be my gym teacher this morning?!" said Phil excitedly.

"Yes, you're coming with Turk apparently, so, we can head to the beach right away if you'd like."

"I've never really worked out before, except for our lame training here, but I just kind of run around the village sometimes because I just feel like it, you know? I need to free the energy in me." And he made a dramatic gesture with his arm showing his energy spreading all around him as if it was leaking out of his body.

"Well, I hope you'll like it then. Turk, I thought you would complain and say you did not need to exercise or that it would be too easy, or, you know, be your annoying self!"

The truth was Turk was happy to only spend half of the morning in the kitchen today as the day before hadn't gone as he'd expected. Besides, he needed the exercise. He was very active back in Robat and if the four Robatians wanted to keep up the strength they'd built over the decades of intense training, they had to do more than just these two hours twice a week. Indarra got to swim two hours everyday plus she was gonna be a stunt double and Tom had to teach four hours a day so they were fine. However, the twins would be standing in the kitchen or acting which did not result in much muscle building. So far, stirring bouillon had been their hardest cardio in Robart!

Anyway, enough discussing their BMI, they took their yoga mats and a few pairs of dumbbells from the closet by the school and set up on the beach. Tom saw Indarra walking a good 15 meters behind Jack and then saw them climb on the rocks that formed the reef around the lagoon.

"Alright, in a couple of months we will start working each muscle group, but for now I just want you to learn more about your own body and develop each of your muscles at your own pace without overloading any of them. I'll make you gain strength and we will work on your cardio before we try to turn you into a big muscle man, like your classmate here."

The twins were both really fit but they were still rather thin so Turk took offense at the comment and was ready to make Tom pay!

"We have two hours which is way too long for an intense workout, so we'll only have 20 minutes of high-intensity work out. This is how this is gonna go: we will stretch for 10, warm up for 15, then we'll try to work every body part, then burn fat with a high-intensity workout and then stretch again and do some yoga. Let's start with warming up."

They started jogging on the beach, did sit-ups, dead-lifts, push-ups, squats, and many other exercises but Phil did not seem to tire of exercising or speaking, to Tom's annoyance. Turk started throwing sand at Tom when he turned his back on them. Phil got the joke and it seemed he would be a great practical joke companion to the twins.

"OK, let's refocus as we're only half-way through," said Tom trying to get control of his class.

"Come on, Tom," complained Turk, "can we take a break? We've been so good for an hour."

"You can take a break once your two hours are over!"

Tom did not manage to keep his students interested really long and before he could do anything, Phil and Turk were in the ocean throwing water at each other and trying to drown one another.

"Hey, boys, could you please go somewhere else, you're scaring my fish away," laughed Indarra who was being hugged by one of the largest squids they had ever seen.

"Do you need a hand with that?" asked Turk.

"No, I'm good, he just likes me a lot!" Indarra tried to say something else but one of the tentacles found its way around her mouth.

After the workout, Tom got two new students and Turk, Indarra, and Phil headed to the showers.

"So, Phil, where do you work?" asked Indarra on the way to the bathroom.

"I fix up houses here. There are a lot of them so I refurbish them one by one and then once I'm done, I start all over again, well, that's what the previous person was doing anyway . . ."

"Oh, right, someone does that job back in Robat, too."

Meanwhile in the fields . . .

"Artea, no time for reveries!" said Adimen in her usual bossy know-it-all voice. "You know we have to gather food for two days instead of one today as the forum staff and field staff will be going to the other village. OK, bring that tray of mushrooms and I'll keep collecting these peppers. This trip will disturb all our organization plus we have no time to work on improving the system. This is really unfortunate and not a good start I'm telling you."

Artea rolled his eyes and walked away at a fast pace towards the forum. He slowed down once he was out of sight.

"Hey, Artea!" said Indarra who was coming back from the beach. "Thanks for bringing everything so quickly."

"No problem, the rest is coming soon. Are you guys alright to cook for two days?" said Artea as he dropped a couple boxes on the kitchen counter.

"Yeah, it will all work out. Curry will be served both days and the grilled fish, well, they'll have to have fish soup again, for another two days." Indarra paused for a second and then said, "Adimen must be unbearable right now!"

"Well, let's say that you'll get everything earlier than planned . . ."

"She means well, she, err, has self-discipline, and expects the same from others, you know, which is a little difficult for anyone who is not a machine."

They both started laughing.

"OK, I better get back or she'll start public whipping me with corn." Artea walked out giving himself little slaps on the butt.

"Alright, we have all four pots running," said Indarra while lifting one of the lids. "We have the extra mushrooms for the curry, now all we need is for sweet Tatiana to bring us the extra minced meat. However, given there's no preparation needed for it and it cooks in five minutes, that's not a problem. Let's work on those mushrooms and somehow we will be good. I'll work on a food plan on the mountain tomorrow since we have no time today and need to get everything ready now for the next two days. That means four huge pots full to the top for four meals and breakfast ready for two days. I want the coffee machine full of coffee beans and each pile of cutlery labeled so they know where to help themselves. Perry, please ask your brother to roll today's cart of dirty dishes into the walk-in fridge tomorrow after breakfast because otherwise, it will start to smell. Am I forgetting anything?" She pointed at things here and there and made a small check sign with her finger every time she was satisfied until . . . "Crap! Dessert! Oh, no, Adimen!" she said with less enthusiasm than before. "Can someone . . . ?" she looked around her and found that all of her kitchen mates had suddenly found something to do. "OK, I'll go . . ."

An hour later, everything was ready, everyone was in the forum for lunch, and Indarra was really happy with the way everything had gone. Perry was certainly happy that with Indarra in the kitchen, he could rest a little bit more. It was like having an easier version of Adimen around.

"Everyone excited about taking their first steps into the movies?" asked Artea, finally excited about an afternoon activity. "Turk, Ross, you're gonna be great as actors, I can't wait to see that!" Although, he may have been half joking about that.

"How is this gonna go?" asked Indarra.

"Well, after lunch, we're gonna meet in the cinema. We'll gather and they will introduce their project. The script will be given to everyone, actors will have to rehearse their lines, and the director will keep an eye on it and see if it's performed as he wants it. Then Tina and Victor will have meetings at different times with the movie set people, stunts, musicians, and so on until we're ready to shoot the first scenes! It usually takes a few months, we have a screening, and start over with a new movie! Speaking of which, let's go!"

Everyone walked to the beach towards the cinema and sat down. Tina and Victor were standing facing the audience and for the first time, Tina looked very serious, concentrated and weirdly sober.

"Welcome everyone!" started Victor. "I would like to start by thanking you for the great work you've done on recreating this terrible historical event. You all worked really hard for the past six months and it was challenging in terms of special effects and the size of the movie set, but above all, because it touched us very much and will remain forever a dark day for us here in Robart. May this movie also honor the memory of little Teddy and Vicky."

Indarra searched around really quickly to find out if someone reacted to those names but she did not pick up on anything. There were no casualties from the wave in the other two villages and accidental death was not a frequent occurrence.

"So, for the next movie," started Tina with a much steadier voice than usual, "we wanted to have fun rather than another real-life tragedy. We wanted to find something fictional and entertaining. But also, with the experience we got from the last movie, we wanna go further with special effects and want to be able to create a place, a place which would not be this one but something foreign. So, this movie will be about other villages coming to visit us from the sky and the other side of the coral reef, where the sharks live."

"They will come on the water on floating machines and in air floating machines," continued Victor. "At first, they will be welcomed with mistrust but then we will learn to live with them. There will be a twist at the end; we will try to shoot it secretly so that a minimum number of people know about it. We will also try to separate tasks as much as possible so that only Tina and I will know the whole story until we ultimately screen the movie and you can all see it!"

"Victor and I started drawing storyboards, starting with the water and air floating machines We thought we could all work on that somehow. Everyone can draw their own idea of what it would look like and then we will decide what we like best, or just get inspired by a few and then mix them into one. We do want the air and water machines to be different as they will not come from the same villages, so they have no reason to be too similar. These are ours."

Tina and Victor pulled out a board with a few draw-ings of absurdly shaped objects. There was one boat that looked like a round platform at the end of a stick. In a different drawing, they had gone further and it turned out that this was the central pillar that linked the other half of the ship, which was once again a circular floor at the end of the pillar but this time underwater. It could not float, nor effectively pierce through water but they did not know that. The aircraft was just as odd. One of them was just a larger bungalow with wings, which was obviously inspired by the wings of the birds they had seen in the village. Another one was more bird shaped and looked freakishly like an actual plane with windows on the side; the wings just looked way too small for its thick body.

"What would the people look like?" interrupted Adimen.

"Hmm who?" asked Victor a little bit surprised that he had been interrupted during his presentation.

"The air and water people, what would they look like?" she repeated.

"I do not think they had to look different; they're just people, living elsewhere, like you guys. You don't look dif-ferent," replied Victor a little bit annoyed but convinced he had ended the exchange.

"Actually we do and the Robatians have a lot more muscle mass than the rest of us, and you'd think that people living in the sky or on water would probably display different features to adapt to their environment. I'm surprised you didn't think of it."

Victor had a growing look of exasperation on his face and looked like he might jump at Adimen's throat. "Well, Adimen," he said over articulating each syllable of her name. "The water people come from a different land, maybe rather similar to ours, so they would have no reason to look different. However, we will see about the people that come from the air. Perhaps they just float over to us from a different land just like ours. Anyway, we're not at the presentation yet and all these things will be explained and further discussed in smaller groups so that we can all bring ideas to this project at appropriate times."

This, of course, concluded Adimen's unwanted interruption.

"We have a few designs for the other two places, but this is not set in stone either," announced Tina. "We thought it would make sense if the water people took on building a machine to explore the waters surrounding them because they lack space and need to expand! We had a few designs in mind; one with a mountain at the back just like here but the flatland would be basically just the beach so there would not be much room for agriculture. This would have forced them to build wall-less bungalow structures but on different levels to grow food, the same for housing and so on. The other design would be more of a small flat circle and they would have started building large piers over the water to extend their living space."

The Robartians all nodded approvingly each and every time she pulled out a new board.

"You need sun for them to grow," muttered Adimen.

"We are not sure about the air people yet," said Victor, "but we thought they could come from a land like this too. One of them could come from the small beach one and the other from the flat one. If you have a more exotic idea, we'd be keen to hear it. Last, we thought of an upside down place, which would sort of mirror ours. It would be a place that we can't see because it's beyond the blue in the sky, but if you elevated far enough you could reach the other land. We want it to look a bit different from this as there is no reason for it to look exactly like Robart. We thought we could actually build a full-sized set for this particular place. Maybe we could shoot outside of the studios and pimp Robart into something different with extra floors but nothing permanent or too complicated. We would just build the outside and only the walls we really needed to, then the inside shoots would be done from the studios so as not to disturb our village life too much. This is a huge project and we'll have a few major movie sets like the two villages, the air floating and floating machines, inside, and outside. We also want to be able to show the machines while they're in motion, which means we need shots in the sky for one and in the water for the other. This implies playing with camera angles or removing our village digitally or dumping the floating one straight into the water with the sharks. However, I am not sure we could get it back safely, but it would make it even more realistic as you'd expect to see sharks since it's out of the lagoon."

"We'll need people to work on the outfits and I'm sure Louis could take care of that," said Tina. "We thought we could use some of our old clothes and mix and match them with some of the costumes from our underwater scenes from that movie we shot a few years back. What was it called?" Tina looked around for help but no one seemed to remember. "It will be tremendous work, more detailed than ever done before, and we will even create cutlery for each place. We thought if everyone was OK with it, that we could customize our actual ones now to make it simpler, and it would be fun to have different—"

"What about the climate?" interrupted Adimen once again.

"The what this time?" asked Victor with his jaw clenched.

"The climate!" stated Adimen matter-of-factly. "There are hypotheses that if we were located somewhere else in the ocean, the weather and temperatures could be very different because of our position from the sun and the presence of different winds . . . these are just hypothesis, but if we're going to create drastically different places, we want to strike it from every angle. As you witness in our freezers when the temperature drops below zero degrees, water turns into ice. It would be interesting if one of the villages experienced this kind of cold temperature. It would also mean they would experience frozen rainfall which could probably damage their houses and put their lives in danger. We could then create the villages accordingly with some safety aspects in mind. If I had to brainstorm off the top of my head," she scratched her head pretending that the following idea had flourished in the four and half second window, "I'd say that while we experience wind storms here, theirs could be stronger, for instance. This could make for a fun and interesting alternative."

Victor was forced to agree that all of these were great ideas while Tina just nodded and smiled at nothing in particular and then decided it was her turn to speak again.

"The cast will be massive and everyone will play their own role here, but will also have to play the roles of the people from the other villages. We will try to make it work so that whoever has a big role in one village will have a small part in the other two and we will make them look like a different person, unless," Tina emphasized the last word a little bit more than she probably needed to, "we can get people from the other two villages and this time I mean the real ones where you guys come from. If by any chance, by then, we have met them."

"This brings us to the next big topic of the day. For this, I would like Artea to come to the stage," said Victor.

⊣⊫

Ross woke up feeling absolutely terrified that morning. He also felt guilty for letting Indarra go up that mountain by herself. Part of him managed to convince himself he had not followed her or stopped her because she had been so convincing and rational about it. However, another part of him knew he was lying to himself and petrified at the idea of even getting close to that mountain; so much so that he had let someone he cared for walk to what was probably her death. What he did not know was that as he was getting out of bed, Indarra, and Tom were actually waking up in a comfortable bed on the other side of the mountain after their rather hostile welcome from Adimen. He would not know this for another couple of days. After a few minutes of not knowing what to do with himself, he finally got up and went downstairs to find his brother already seated there.

"Hey there!" said Turk seeing his brother coming down the stairs. "Ready for a first great day under Deborah's regime?"

"Oh, man, what happened?"

"I went outside to get us some food – it's 11:30 AM by the way and you totally overslept! Anyway, seeing that Indarra and Tom were gone, she figured she could somehow take control. She's given everyone jobs they didn't necessarily want, or the one they've been somehow trained for, as much as we have been trained, of course . . ."

"Let me guess."

"Yep, you guessed right . . ."

"Sneaky bitch! Anyway, we can fight back and reclaim control, can't we? I don't wanna mop floors for the rest of my life!"

"Well, there's no reclaiming anything," said Turk, "as no one ever had control. What we really need to do is to do is put her back in her place."

They heard muffled voices coming from the beach.

"Do you hear that?" Ross asked.

They walked out of their house and saw Deborah standing on a chair on the beach with Melissa on the sand beside her. She was trying to gather everyone to give a speech. One could say that Deborah already had a rather disgraceful face, but seeing her from under made it even worse, thought Turk. Most of the village was now there even though no one seemed to really want to be, however, as they were all very confused it was certainly easier to have someone make the decisions for them, even if that person was Deborah. She knew that and if she was gonna have her moment of glory, it was now because later Indarra might return or the Robatians' morale could improve and they would realize they didn't need her after all. And Melissa? Well, she was just along for the ride. No moment would probably ever be her moment, but it was as close as it would get so she stood next to Deborah proudly, feeling like this victory was somehow hers too – FYI, it was not.

Just to be clear, It was not exactly as if Deborah had some-how managed to gather everyone there thanks to her charisma or because she was liked by the crowd, but once someone starts standing on a chair on a beach and calling out for people to come along, well, naturally a few people will come along. Then, if you walk by and notice a gathering, others will want to get closer and see what it's all about. Turk and Ross did not technically take part in the gathering. They just observed it from afar, sitting on their front porch and taking in the scene from their property. Deborah was still gesturing in every direction, like a marionette that the operator did not know how to operate. At this point, she was probably gesturing into nothingness as there weren't that many people left in the village. She was frustrated the twins hadn't appeared at her feet. She wasn't going to actually call out their names as it would show the rest of the crowd that some of them were quietly protesting and that was the last thing she needed. So, after gesturing some more, she finally started her speech.

"My fellow Robatians, yesterday was unfortunate, destabilizing, confusing, and frustrating to say the least, but today is a new day, and we can't let this tragic event take us down. We need to act rationally and start organizing ourselves for the good of the community. There is one thing we will not do," she paused for dramatic effect, "and that it is to cowardly leave our village. Whether it is to die or any other stupid reason, no! I will not let this happen again. Instead, we will stay here and do what needs to be done. Do you think our ancestors built this community on selfishness, by doing the job that made them happy? By taking breaks whenever they felt like it? No, they created this fantastic place, our legacy," and she paused again and invited everyone to look at the village behind them by showing it with her hand. "Your legacy!" she added while showing each Robatian with the palm of her hands as if she was starting a cult. "They made this community great by acting selflessly, by following rules, by doing what they were told for the good of the community, and it worked. Look at what we have now: the beautiful houses we

live in and the technologies we have mastered. Do we want it to be all for nothing? Could we live with ourselves knowing that we're the generation that let it all go to its end? Believe in me, follow me, and you will not have to carry this burden. Let me do it for you. I have stayed up all night, redistributing tasks, creating jobs, and perfecting a system so that everyone can contribute to our society and feel like they deserve their place here. I will be using the school as an office from now on, you can find me there for guidance, but today, I will need you to come by one by one so you can get your schedule and understand how you can earn your place in Robat. My dear friends, I promise you a bright future here in Robat."

She finally stepped down from her chair and started pointing at people one by one, telling them in which order they could come and visit her in the school for their private guidance. it was probably by order of their social ranking in her society. Once she had finished on the beach, she gave the twins' house a really cold look and finally acknowledged their existence. Then she pointed at them back and forth making her nasty little finger move forward and back really fast, trying to summon them.

The twins went back inside but did not really know what to do with their day. School was no longer a thing and although that did not bother them it had broken their routine. Everyone always longed for more free time, but once you have it you don't remember why you wanted it in the first place. You think there are so many things you wanna do like learn new crafts but once the moment actually happens, well, to be honest, we are usually all pretty lazy. Weirdly, the twins decided they would actually head to the kitchen and take care of lunch as it was something they felt comfortable with; they had hung out in the kitchen as children and helped out the cooks whenever they had managed to sneak out of school. The cooks always let them watch what they were doing for a little while before sending them back to school making them promise never to do it again. However, once a week or so, they would manage to escape in between classes and enter the forum to attend to their favorite hobby, whether it was skipping school or cooking, nobody knows!

"Do you think we'll be able to cook two whole meals by lunchtime? I mean," Ross paused for a moment, "we used to just help out a little, and that was years ago."

"My dear brother," started Turk confidently. "I think you've forgotten that I am amazing!"

"Oh, right, this must have been the piece of information I was missing," said Ross smirking at his brother. "So, should we make our famous mushy peas to piss off Indarra?"

"What would be the point?" replied Turk. "She is not even here to be pissed off. Let's wait for her to get back and we'll make braised ladybirds."

Both laughed but they felt very uncomfortable about it all. Ross was probably trying to bring her up to see if his brother was worried too, but just the fact that her absence was this taboo clearly proved that he reciprocated the feeling.

"OK, let's see what they have in here." Ross started going through fridges and cabinets and pulled out a few things.

"I guess Deborah was not that efficient at finding people to bring food here. Isn't that her job?" asked Turk.

"Well, we'll have to make do with what we have. There's plenty of pasta so we could just make a sauce with the eggplants and they'll have to like it!"

"OK, but then we have to make them pasta soup for dinner and all we have left is tap water. If we're going to earn our place in the kitchen that's gonna be a big fail . . . How about we just cook lunch and wait for the barn and field team to bring us ingredients in the afternoon?"

"You know what," said Ross suddenly feeling a rush of confidence in him, "the hell with her! We're gonna show her and all of them that we can do everything, including their jobs!" Ross stopped for a second, sort of looking upon himself from the outside without understanding who this new Ross was. But he liked him and figured he wouldn't stick around for long so he might as well get the best out of him.

"Well, maybe not too much! If we are too amazing at everything I'm scared they will overload us with work and I still wanna have time to be awesome at chilling."

"Turk, go to the silo and get tomatoes, broccoli, peas, and cauliflower. I'll head to the farm and drag a whole pig here if I have to," said Ross ignoring his brother's silliness. "Meet you here in 10."

They both returned a bit later with all the ingredients and cooked two fantastic meals for the village and even finished on time, at about 12:15 PM. They noticed they had forgotten dessert so they both headed back to the silo to get fruit, thinking they could probably whip up a quick fruit salad, but by the time they got back everyone was already in the forum. Deborah was standing over the stove looking at the pots full of food with her hands on her hips. "Who made this?" she asked when the twins entered the forum.

"We made it," said Ross proudly, "we have lunch and dinner ready and we'll need food brought in today so that we can focus on cooking tomorrow and not have to also go out to get the food from the back of the village."

Deborah was speechless. She wanted to tell the twins off for performing a chore not assigned to them but thought it might come back to bite her. However, she was not easy to destabilize. "And why would you do that? I don't see how you could have cooked and performed your actual job!"

"This is our actual job! Weren't you supposed to do yours too, because it looks like we ended up doing it for you!" said Ross getting red in the face.

"I've been doing my job all morning. I'm taking care of the village and there are frozen lasagnas in the freezer so no one needed to cook today or get food from the barn and the silo. What we needed was for you two to do your job and now the rest of the village is going to suffer for it. We could have been living in a clean place, but nooooo!" she said lingering on the o. "You thought you could do what made you happy even if the rest of the village had to pay for your selfishness."

"Well, we did not know and we don't wanna clean," said Turk who was not making the point he thought he was.

"Melissa, stick the lasagnas in the oven." Deborah pointed at her lame friend without making eye contact with her. "How about we all head upstairs for a drink in the meantime. It's a beautiful day and we get to enjoy it."

"What about what we cooked? You aren't just gonna . . ." started Ross but she was already half-way up the stairs. "Turk, grab a pot and I'll get the other one. We cooked it so it's ours!"

They headed back to their house with enough food for a really long time. Funnily enough, despite having kitchens in their houses for no reason, they finally gave it a purpose. Little did they know that in Robat, at the same time, the same thing was happening for Tom and Indarra in Adimen's house.

They had food for 40 people but hardly ate anything for lunch. They just wandered around the house, purposeless, until Ross spoke up.

"We need to go get them. You know, Tom is gone too," he added as if to make sure it mattered to his brother. "I say we leave tomorrow morning, at first light. We sneak out and head to the mountain. Maybe they fell and got hurt and they need help."

"Or they were eaten alive the second they stepped on that mountain and so will we if we go there," said Turk.

"Brother! You know we have to do the right thing." Ross looked at Turk with a smile but he really meant that they had to get their act together.

"I hate you! You're right . . . Why do you get to be the nice one and I have to be the handsome one? It's just so unfair!" said Turk.

Ross smacked him gently, or not so gently depending on who you ask. Why did not they tell Indarra and Tom that they had planned to come to save them? It's probably one of those times when someone does something great even though you had the idea first, but if you come up and say you were about to do it you just look like a jerk. So somehow they picked coward over jerk!

"Ross, I think we need to pack up and maybe get sticks to protect ourselves."

"Or maybe a fishing net to trap whatever is out there?" Ross stopped. "Is that her again?"

It seemed like Deborah was up on her chair again so the twins opened their door to see what was going on. They saw

Melissa on a chair this time, but she was not using it as a throne or a pedestal, she was hammering a board onto the school wall. The twins approached and started reading. It was a list of official jobs and their schedule to which she had added at the bottom in capital letters:

ANYONE WHO FAILS TO FULFILL THEIR DUTIES IS AN ENEMY OF OUR SOCIETY AND WILL BE SHUNNED.

Chapter 9

WHY BE SALTY WHEN YOU CAN BE IN ROBART!

"Hello, everyone," said Artea when he stepped up onto the stage next to Victor. "As you all know, we've had guests for the past two days and these five great people have befriended us all very quickly. They say they come from another two villages on the other side of the mountain. This is the mountain we all thought shaped the boundaries of our world and was dangerous and uncrossable. Against all odds, after the catastrophe that hit us all a few days ago, a group of brave people from Robat decided to head into the mountains to find the First Generation that also went missing from their village.

"One of them thought she heard their voices in the mountain, but as it turned out what she had heard were our screams of shock when we woke up to a village where more than half of the population had vanished overnight. They risked their lives to save who they thought was their parents, but instead, they saved us. They saved us from an ignorance and seclusion we were not ready for. Sadly, the other two villages have not been lucky enough to be part of this incredible discovery. They are still living in fear, wondering where these five people are and where their parents are. Each of these villages has their own habits and knowledge. A knowledge we can share with one another in hope of a better future. That is why, tomorrow, a group of eight people will head to both villages to let them know their friends are alive and that we are here, ready to welcome them if they ever want to visit."

People started talking between themselves, quietly at first and then louder.

"I understand this may worry you," continued Artea, "but I assure you there's no reason to feel unsafe."

"How can you assure us of that? You have not met them and for all we know it could be a trap," shouted Tatiana.

"Well, that's a risk I am ready to take and that the other seven people in this mission are also ready to take. Don't forget that we have been hosting Indarra, Tom, Adimen, Ross, and Turk for two days and we've all got to know them. They are not dangerous."

"Who said you could make decisions here? Why are you in charge all of a sudden?" asked Tatiana in disgust.

"I am not in charge of anything and I am not the head of the mission. Actually, I am only a tool or something, but you're right, I do not make decisions for the whole group as we do not do that here. I am making a decision for myself. I was invited to this mission and I agreed to go. It might end up having repercussions for you on some level, but so does everything else we do here. I am not doing anything wrong and neither are the other seven. One thing we cannot do though is forbid people from circulating about the land as they wish to, whether it is within the boundaries of our village or beyond. Anyone is free to visit these villages if they feel like it, as long as it's peaceful. They're free to come here too, as our five friends did. We just thought that the first visit should be an organized one, as it will come as a shock to everyone. This is why this is a planned mission composed of people they know and trust and of people from other villages so they can meet and learn about us for themselves. From now on, our lives will become a lot more interesting. Aren't you all curious to know more about these people and where they're from?"

Tatiana and Roger, her fellow butchering companion, got up and left after cursing Artea who pretended not to be destabilized by it.

Indarra stood up next to Artea. "I understand your reticence. I was really scared when I first stepped foot on the mountain. I thought I would die but I was so desperate as I believed my family needed me. You guys have a great thing going on here and I get that you don't want it to be ruined by taking a risk, which might degrade your happiness. I cannot promise you that this mission will bring happiness to everyone here, but I honestly think that it won't make anyone less happy. I don't know much about Robin, but I now know Adimen, and she is my friend, I know that if the people she grew up with are only half as amazing and witty and smart and faithful a friend as she is, well, then I don't wanna wait another minute to meet them because I want them in my life too. And I think that this is what this mission is all about."

Everyone seemed to have either gotten their mind around the idea or even become really excited, except for Tatiana and Roger; but to be honest, he probably didn't have a chance to voice his own opinion.

"Alright everyone," said Victor. "Now that all of this is clear, let the fun begin. Let's go back to the movie. First, we will pick what the places will be like as a general idea and brainstorm. I want it to go fast, no over thinking, so let's just jump straight into it. Whether you like our ideas and wanna pick one of them or maybe you have something better, we're ready to hear it. We will all draw what we think is the best look for these places and bring those sketches to James, Tom, Phil, and Adimen, who will ultimately decide as they will be designing every room, every machine, and everything you will see in the movie. Louis will start on designing the clothes once he knows more about their environment. One of us will be in charge of casting; this is a big job, as we will all be acting in at least two different roles each. We will have our main acting crew of Jerry, Jack, Veronica, Ross, Turk, Tatiana, and Roger. They will have to work closely with the director and that is also true of Artea and Indarra's stunt team. Thankfully, this year we will have both a male and female stunt person. Artea, you won't have to wear wigs anymore – how sad!"

Everyone laughed.

"OK, I'll let you read the script and I will come back in two hours, you'll get to tell me all your ideas."

Victor, Tina, Artea, and Indarra stepped down from the podium and everyone started talking within their own group.

"Thank you," said Adimen to Artea and Indarra. "Really, thank you. I appreciate everything that is being done and what has been said," she said shyly looking at her feet.

"Please, all of this is making me happy, to be honest. I mean, I miss my family, but I was already used to that," Artea said the end of the sentence more quietly. "I never thought that I belonged here and always thought it had other possibilities and that there was so much more we could do. I always thought I was inadequate and our whole existing living space was so limited. I always dreamed of visiting faraway lands, bigger than this one, with more people and more things to do. Also, I am sick of all this painting and working on other useless crafts. I like being more active. I wish I could walk for hours you know and see things. I don't know how to explain it, but I wish the landscape could change as I walk." He laughed. "I always thought that maybe there was more to life and now I know that it's true all I wanna do is see it and start doing different things with different people. I want a new life, I wanna meet someone new, someone special, someone who clearly is not here right now. Adimen, I actually do like your practical way of seeing things and the way you can intellectualize things. We don't really do that here, it's only about the beauty of things," he said making a face as if he was smelling old cheese. "And you guys," he added looking at the Robatians, "I like how you don't bother with the little things and you're so out-doorsy and free. I have been exercising in my room every morning because I needed it. The short biweekly sports class we have has never been enough for me. I envy you,

Indarra. I would love to work as a fisher but I'm not great underwater sadly. Anyway, how do you guys feel about the movie?"

"Well, it's weirdly similar to real life even though they said they did not want something historical, to make it more fun. However, somehow, it's happening now," said Indarra matter-of-factly.

"Actually, this topic was requested a few months ago when the movie about the wave was announced. People wanted something fun, entertaining, about lands outside of ours, but the First Generation did not seem to like the topic so it was set aside. I guess Victor and Tina worked on it anyway and now the First Generation is gone, they decided to pull it out. There's no way she wrote a 200-page script about you guys arriving here in 48 hours so it's just a random coincidence. So, do you guys have any new ideas about what the villages could be like?"

"I stand by the fact that one of them should experience temperatures below 0 degrees as it could make for a really interesting plot," said Adimen.

"I like the idea that one of them comes from the sky, but the upside down thing is a little weird though," said Ross. "What if what we see as blue sky is the bottom of their sea and that's why it's blue, so they'd have to go around the edges of their sea and down to us!"

Unbelievable as it seemed, Ross' idea was chosen. One village would be set on a frozen land in the sky while the other village would be on the other side of the sea, which is why they came on "floating machines." The village that was located on the other side of the sea, would be the one with limited space. They went for the small flat land version, not the one with the mountain, to make it different from Robart. It would have a long strip of sand with buildings of several floors and piers out on the water to compensate for the lack of space. Adimen maintained that the idea was ridiculous and that you could not grow food on several floors even without walls because they would lack light, but as they told her, "it is just a movie!"

"Adimen, your ideas were just brilliant. I can't tell you how impressed I was and there is so much you can bring to this project. We have wanted to make a movie that did not take place here for a very long time so it's a big moment for all of us. A large section will take place here, of course, but still, there will be four sets! Can you believe it? Four!" said Phil with a tone of excitement that bordered on madness.

"Four?" asked Adimen confused.

"Of course! There will be the two new villages and the sets which will demonstrate the journeys across the sea and from the sky. That's four different sets. How about I show you how we do things here! OK, so some things are clearly ours to do. For instance, if we decide that we need to make the air floating machines completely CGI, then it will be our job, but for the water ones, we will probably end up building them. Let's say that one of our jobs overlaps with Tom and James a little bit. Ultimately, they will decide what the machines look like, but we are the ones who need to make them float and who must manage to take them from point A to point B or if we decide that they need to get destroyed for the plot of the movie. This is something that we'll have to work on, you see?"

"Yeah, I think I get it. Also, I don't think they should be called air floating machines but simply flying machines, just the same way birds fly! Anyway, how about the frozen land?" asked Adimen.

"Well, it will depend on the way we do the scenes. I guess scenes with wide angles will be ours to work on. We'll CGI the crap out of Robart and make it white, change the buildings, and they can also build a maquette. Then they'll only need us to add the sky, water, and maybe give a few effects . . . For close up shots, we'll probably have to make it indoor and make everything look icy with practical special effects so the four of us will work together. Let's say they decide what the walls should look like and build them, we'll make them icy. See, sometimes the border between our jobs is small, but we usually work it out, and James is amazing anyway so it's fun working with him. What should we start with?"

"I have a few ideas," said Adimen feeling right in her element. "For the floating device, I am not sure how big they want them but they probably want it to sustain the weight of a few people and maybe even food and beds if the trip is long. Either way, I think there is a standard design that will work regardless of the size. We could make something float if we filled it with air, or did not let water in. It should basically be a box that does not let water in, you see? We studied friction where I am from and if you want it to move in the water it will need minimum friction so the shape can't be squared. I think a circle would be better but it should be more like an oval." Adimen grabbed a sheet of paper. "Do you have a pen? I'll show you."

"That sounds like a great idea," said Phil while searching through drawers. "You see, that's exactly our job here, you've really got it. Now, it's time for the experiments. We will go to the ocean, start with small models, and see what happens. We have been storing loads of wooden boards from previous movie sets so we can use them."

Adimen followed Phil to the back of the studios. There were at least 10 doors going to different rooms, closets, and other storage spaces. James opened one of them and they picked up a few of the wooden boards that were neatly stacked against a wall. They carried them to a table in the studios, sawed, measured, and sawed some more for a while until they got the oval-shaped boards Adimen had imagined. To these, they nailed vertical boards, which kind of made it look like an oval-shaped camembert box without the lid. Once Adimen was satisfied with the result, they walked to the beach and got knee deep in the ocean.

"Hmm," started Adimen, pushing it around in the water. "There is still a lot of friction; I think the front needs to be pointy to break through the water."

They went back to the studios and started over but this time they made it too skinny and too tall so the structure was not stable anymore. On the fifth attempt, they seemed to find the perfect ratio of height, width, weight, and length.

"Yes, we made it. Yes!" screamed Adimen in a way that was almost hysterical and so unlike her. "Err," she started thinking out loud, "I guess once we add more weight, people, walls, and furniture on top of it, it could be that we will have to make it a little wider. I guess we should try now before we build a full-size version. To be honest, we don't know yet what it will look like, but let's say that the movie set team will have to understand that we have shape restrictions since it needs to float. It would be interesting to go and tell them about the possibilities before they start designing things which won't work . . ."

They agreed and walked over to James and Tom who were already working on the boats.

"OK, James, sorry to kill your creativity, but it seems like your floating tower is not going to be a thing, it just won't float. It needs to be flatter as a tall shape will just fall on its side. Take a look at this model we made; it's the ideal shape we found after making several other alternatives."

"OK," said James who seemed bothered by the news. "That's too bad, see, since they are really into having different levels in that village, we thought it would have been built vertically."

"Well, I guess there is another option," started Adimen, "but it would be complicated and really hard to maneuver. I'll walk you through it. If we add enough weight at the bottom of the floating structure, we could submerge it completely, then the tall structure could be on top of it, but for the machine to be tall and still habitable, we would need it to be at least five meters by five for it to fit people comfortably." She calculated using her fingers and the air in front of her as a board. "Yeah, that's what I thought. If we want it to be three stories; that is five by five meters and three meters high for each floor, we need to make the submerged structure about one meter high, by, I think, at least 25 meters. If we were to pull it with a rope to make it look like it moves by itself, then we would basically need all the inhabitants of two villages just to pull it. This is nerve-wracking," she said in absolute distress. "OK, thankfully I brought books with me but I will clearly need to get some more tomorrow when I am in Robin. Maybe, if we thicken the superstructure, we can make it shorter and lighter, but then I am not sure it would be stable. Hmm, I have seen Phil swim and I don't think you want this thing to topple over while he is on the top floor or you might have to recruit a new actor," she said matter-of-factly.

Everyone started laughing but soon realized that she was not mocking Phil but instead, she was so focused on her work that she was not actually bothered that Phil might get hurt. Casting a new actor could delay production time and that was unacceptable.

"I know!" she said louder than needed and startled everyone. "We could drop a few stones at the bottom of it and it would help us with balance, but good luck maneuvering it. Then again, we're not actually crossing the ocean with it so stability is the priority. It's decided – that is how it will be done. I'll give you the construction details by tomorrow morning so you can start building it while we're on our way to the other villages."

She left without looking at anyone, still gesturing with her hand and making calculations while the other three stood there confused about what had just happened.

Apparently, as talented as Adimen was, the work dispatch concept was not something she had comprehended.

Meanwhile, on a roof nearby . . .

"OK, this time it was too soft. I told you to relax your knees not to turn them into melting butter. That was better but you really need to let your knees absorb the shock. They need to bend and then you roll on your side," said Artea a little amused.

"OK, OK, I think I got it," said a bleeding Indarra. Both her arms were completely bruised and her lip was cracked open and swollen. She climbed up the ladder again onto the roof of one of the bungalows and watched Artea once again as he jumped off the roof with ease and confidence.

"See I push with my legs, land soft, move left, and roll." He got up with pride.

Once Indarra's elbows were actually damaged nearly to the bone, she finally got it and felt like the experience was really rewarding.

"You know, of course, I need to train you to be a stunt model, but you have a lot to teach me too."

"Really, like what?" asked Indarra surprised.

"Well, you guys are used to physical activities, but above all, you seem to be great in the water. I hate to admit it but I suck at water related stuff. I am actually terrified of water." He looked away for a second and Indarra saw something in his eyes, but it looked like sadness more than fear. "Indarra, I would love it if you could help me fight my fear of water. Clearly, we will need it for this movie," he added getting himself together.

"Of course, I would love to help you," said Indarra gazing into the eyes of this beautiful man who was strong, and well-built but somehow looked like a child at that very moment. She knew she would never have him, but she had just met who would surely become a friend.

They both walked down to the beach and undressed, watching Adimen running after sheets of paper that had gone flying down the beach from their place under a small rock. Her maquette was also floating away. She did not seem to know if she should get the documents first or get in the water and rescue the maquette.

Indarra laughed and said, "Adimen, get the documents, Artea and I were going in the water anyway so we will bring the maquette back to you."

"Oh, thank you," said Adimen while watching one of the sheets flying over one of the bungalows.

Tina was there and caught it. "Oh, you guys are working on the floating machine!" Tina seemed really impressed. "Good job, guys, I like what you're doing."

"We're not sure yet about safety though," added Adimen in real concern. "See we wouldn't want for someone to get hurt or worse."

"Well, on the upside, if Tatiana dies maybe she'll return as a lovely person, so maybe it's worth a couple of loose nails!" Tom said.

Indarra laughed.

"Come back?" asked Artea a little confused.

"Yes," said Indarra simply.

"What do you mean come back?"

"Come back after she dies."

"Come back after she dies?" asked Artea once again more confused than ever. "Come back from where?"

"You guys don't come back after your death?" asked Indarra surprised and a little sorry for them.

"No, that would be crazy," said Artea. "So, do you remember who you were before?"

"No, that's not how it works," explained Tom not knowing how to explain something that seemed so obvious to him. "You don't remember, but we just know."

"How do you know?" asked Artea a bit doubtful. "You've witnessed it?"

"Err, no," said Indarra a bit confused herself now.

"But you know someone who has witnessed it?" asked Artea again trying to make sense of this.

"No, it's just something we've been told so . . . oh!" and Indarra seemed to put two and two together. "I don't even wanna think about it."

"I find it a little self-obsessed that you cannot picture our village without you in it," said Tina making everyone shut up.

Once this little incident was over and everything had been retrieved, Artea walked slowly towards the sea. Indarra dove straight into the water and felt the pain of the salt starting to eat off the flesh where she had hurt herself jumping from the roof, but she was happy to be in the water. Her feeling of bliss disappeared when she saw the expression in Artea's eyes.

"I can't go further than this," said Artea flatly. He was barely ankle deep.

"It's OK, we don't need to go further. How about we just sit in the water, right there, no need to go further."

At first, he did not move, so she walked back to him and held both his hands facing him and the beach, standing in deeper water than him. She started bending her knees while looking at him and smiled. "See, it's not too bad although it's going to sting like crazy if you've got wounds like me but otherwise it is just really pleasant. Come one!" she said with a naughty smile. "Stick that pretty tushy of yours in there."

He started laughing and relaxed a bit. He did not actually sit all the way down but rather sat on his legs, which was already a big improvement.

"I won't let go of your hands unless you tell me to, Artea, don't worry."

"OK, OK," he said slowly and concentrated as if someone was feeding him rocket ship science about a job he would have to do an hour from now while he was performing brain surgery.

Indarra started letting go but he immediately reacted.

"What do you think you're doing?"

"Err, you said 'OK, OK' so I thought you meant I should let go."

"No, it meant I understood! You're probably going to have to hold my hands for the whole time we're in today."

"I think I like two people at the same time; do you think it's weird?" she asked casually and out of nowhere.

"As in . . . romantically?"

"I am not sure," she paused and looked towards the reef giving herself the time to think. "I mean I love Tom, more than anyone I think, but, yeah, we're just friends and I would not want anything else from him. He already means a lot to me, maybe even more than what you could get from a romantic relationship, but, with Tom, it's safe and easy. I know I have always had him and always will.

Though when it comes to these two people, it is, very different. I have just met one of them and the other one, well, we just really got to know each other this well, since this whole thing happened."

"OK, is that a problem or a good thing? I, for myself, live in a place where I will never be able to be intimate with anyone. There is simply no one I like or and no one for me, so maybe your thing should be celebrated as you have options!"

"It's the salty water talking," she said smiling. "Honestly, so far I have never really thought about it and it really just hit me now. Do people have sex a lot here?"

"Some people, but not much," said Artea. "Have you ever?"

"A few times, but I think the last time I was around 20, so it has been a few years. It has never been something I really felt like doing often, but it has sort of, hmm, come back? For a few days now . . ."

"Me too, actually, it is really weird but I seem to need to do it alone more often and it seems like it is not enough anymore."

"Well, I think Turk would happily give you a hand, or most people I believe, so just go for it!" She winked and pointed down to his private parts with her elbows out and lifted one leg in a grotesque move.

"You would not though I can tell," said Artea, not hurt, almost happily.

"No . . ." she trailed off. "I don't know why because you're probably the most attractive human being I have ever met and yet I don't see you as a sexual entity. Maybe you're just so out of everyone's league that you've actually looped back and out of our sexual spectrum," she said jokily. "Plus, I already have my hands full with my two crushes. I am surprised you did not ask me who these two people were. I would have been more nosy."

"Oh, I am nosy, I just already know who they are!" he said and winked.

"Is it that obvious?" she asked.

"No, I just notice things and that is why I told you that you were lucky for having options because they are options and they both like you too."

"You think so? OK. But you see, the thing is if I choose one I will hurt the other and I kind of want both. Can we do that? Would we be a trouple?"

Artea laughed really hard and just naturally pulled his legs out from under him and fully sat in the water, letting the waves crash on his stomach. "A trouple! I like the idea, so, yes, why not. I don't think we have ever been given rules for any of that stuff, so why not, but then they would have to like each other too."

"Yeah, I think that's where my plan becomes tricky . . ."
They both laughed.

"I am really sorry about your brother," said Indarra.

Artea looked at her a moment and just nodded. Then she smiled, got up, and pulled him on his legs.

"You sexy, muscular piece of meat! I will not let you drown but I will also let you see the good side of water!"

They both smiled.

"I know what we're gonna do. I need to get you to do things that you would not usually do in the water. I noticed you don't have balls here, but tomorrow we'll bring back a couple balls from Robat and I'll teach you how to play water polo. You'll be so entertained you will end up jumping in the water face first without realizing you're actually doing it."

"I'm looking forward to it and I am so happy to go to your village. By the way, I can tell you are trying to make me walk in deeper and deeper while trying to distract me by talking to me!"

"I was not!" said Indarra in false outrage.

"Tell me about your village. I know I will see it tomorrow, but I just can't wait."

"Well, as you know, it is really similar to yours but we live in houses instead of bungalows. We're pretty happy I would say, but something always felt off, like you said,

and now whatever I tell you about it will be wrong somehow because it feels like a lot of it was just built on a lie.
But, you'll meet some nice people and it will be fun. I
mean, I loved discovering this place. I did not see much
of Robin as we were hiding there, but the feeling of discovering new territory is satisfying in a way that can't be
compared with anything else."

"Why were you hiding?"

"I don't really know to be honest; I think it just seemed
like the right thing to do. We actually do have a few shitty
people back home, and Robin, well, they are a bit more,
hmmm, well, you've met Adimen . . ." she was only half-
joking. "It was the first place we visited and everything
was still really chaotic as it was only two days after the
First Generation disappeared. Actually, when I left Robat
I did not tell anyone about it but the twins and Tom, who
followed me. Then we met Adimen, spent a night there,
and decided to go explore. However, first, we returned
to Robat to get the twins, which we did secretly so, no
one saw us. We have our Tatiana and whoever her friend
is back in Robat too, but they are worse I think and I
am scared that, my village is not doing as well as yours. I
have been trying to ignore it, but I feel guilty for being so
happy here, happier than I have ever been really. I wonder
if it is a good thing for you to go with us but on the other

hand, I think we have to! Listen, I am going to tell you something I have never told anyone." She looked around to make sure they were alone.

"There was a woman back in my village, an incredible woman who is actually Tom's mother. We have always had a connection and she dropped a few clues for me to find before they left. See, I'm great at geology, well not Adimen great, but I'm good with whatever basic geology we learned. The day before they disappeared, she handed a test back to us and when she gave it back to me she said she was disappointed that I had failed. However, when I looked at it, I noticed that I had got all the answers right. She was trying to get my attention. On the test, she'd written that such a great student should take those skills from theory to practice. There was also this comment about my underwater abilities, although I still don't really know what she was trying to say. Anyway, she acted strangely a few times. Those clues were supposed to help me and through me, her son as well. I think she knew about the other villages. I can't tell Tom about it, not yet at least, as it would devastate him, but that is why I went over the mountain. She somehow told me to, and I think she gave me clues about the existence of other places. You said you have always suffered and felt you were living in something that was somehow too small for you, this place. Now that we know how large our land is, isn't it weird that a village so small still had a restricted area?"

"You mean the roundhouse?"

"Yeah! Of course, the roundhouse! Why don't you guys go inside?" She said watching Tatiana running up Main Street.

"They just said we could not because it was dangerous and we kind of just never found a reason why we would go in there."

"Well, somehow it was enough to convince you not to. In our village, they just put up cameras around the door and told us that they were dangerous animals who needed to be trained to accept us and people working for the roundhouse had to go through a long training period to have the animals respect them, which in retrospect, we were really stupid to believe something like this. . . This could not work for you as you knew what cameras were since you make movies here. Anyway, isn't it weird that so much crap came out of such a small room? What did they do in there all day? We didn't know what cameras could do but having seen you use them, I am pretty sure they won't jump off the wall and eat off my face as I am also pretty sure the mountain won't eat off my feet. You know what I think? They were hiding something in there and we need to go in there tonight!"

"Should we tell everyone?"

"No! We should not tell anyone! Adimen will wanna plan it for days, the twins will just act silly, and I do not want Tom to know about it because I don't want to tell him about his mom and if we ask the rest of them to tag along then we have to ask Tom."

"How should we do it?"

"Well, Artea, it is just a room and it has a door, a door in front of which we have walked past for years. Somehow, no one has ever been curious to go and open it. I mean we could literally just get you out of the water and be in there in under a minute, but, of course, as everything we do these days, I believe we're gonna have to wait for everyone to fall asleep before we go in. Isn't that easier than being thigh deep in water?"

"I am thigh deep! Well done, Indarra, you are a good teacher!"

"Oh, my dear, it is more than this, trickery and mind control," and she poked his head with a finger giving him a mystical look.

"This t-shirt your wearing, that's not from here is it?" asked Artea grabbing a sleeve.

"No, I got it back from Louis after he washed it. It was really nice of him to remember I came with it."

"Sure. You also have that symbol on your clothes; that triangle cut in three."

"I had never seen it this way, I always thought it was three stripes."

"Oh, yeah maybe."

⊣⊨⊢

A few minutes earlier . . .

"If we do not make a decision quickly the engine might overheat and we will burst into flames. If we wanna make it alive to Robat then we have to get rid of some of the weight!" said Turk dramatically.

"I can't even say my line after this idiot," said Tatiana.

"Well, maybe you should just go back to your barn and torture animals so you won't have to act with me!" said Turk feeling really hurt.

"Cut!" screamed Victor. "We're only rehearsing but once we have the set in place, sometimes you won't get reshoots so Tatiana, control yourself!"

Tatiana left and went towards the back of the village, probably going back to the barn, the only place where she seemed to be happy.

"What is wrong with her!" shouted Turk who was always in a good mood but somehow had found someone who could make him feel like life was not as beautiful as it had always been promised.

"Well, that's just Tatiana," said Victor. "She kind of overreacts, a lot!"

"Yeah, she must be jealous or something because I am not doing anything wrong!"

"Well . . ." started Victor carefully. "It is your first day and you can't master the craft right away!

"What do you mean?" asked Turk feeling as if this was officially the worst day of his life. "What am I doing wrong?"

"Well, there is this thing that a lot of people do at first when they are very confident, it's, err, you know . . ." he paused for a second, "overacting.?" he said trying the word.

"What?"

"Don't worry, it just takes some practice, nothing to worry about. You'll get the hang of it. The trick is to watch yourself act, that's why we tape it all, so you can watch it later and see what you are doing right and what you are doing wrong," said Victor apologetically seeing Turk's sad face. Seeing Ross' amused face, he added. "But don't worry, your brother is doing even worse so. . ."

"What?!" screamed Ross. "I felt so empowered! How can I be worse?"

"Well, good for you, but it always sounds like you've just seen a flying cow and you wanna point it out for other people to see. So, boys, we have some work to do before we actually get to shoot the actual parts of the movie, firstly, because none of the sets are built yet and because everything we shoot with this acting would be garbage. There's no need to cry, no one expected you to be great at it right away. Honestly, watching yourself on the screen will do you some good. Meanwhile, I will talk to Tatiana as I don't think we should try again today. Just watch tapes of yourself and try working together. We'll sleep on it and try again when we're back from the other village." Victor walked out of the studios and headed to the barn leaving the twins feeling, err, well, like shit!

"Can you believe them!" said Turk in indignation. "How dare they say we're bad actors. But you are worse than me, yeah!" He shouted in celebration.

"It is not as fun as I thought it would be, thanks to Tatiana. She is disturbing us with her, err, she is so mean!" said Ross.

"She really is! She really, really is!" he paused for a moment looking at the screen and back at his brother. "Do you think that it's possible we haven't mastered the craft yet? Let's look at the screens. How does it work?" Turk started pushing a bunch of buttons and somehow managed to see their rehearsal.

"We are looking good!" said Turk elbowing his brother.

"Hmmm, OK, I guess we could look more human-like . . ." said Ross. "We might seem let's say, a little too enthusiastic."

"OK, we suck!" declared Turk. "I think they're right, we might have to change a few things. See how Tatiana does it; she doesn't move her arms left and right or speak at the top of her lungs, she just looks natural, like it's a normal conversation. She's really ugly though . . ."

"How is that relevant?"

"I don't know, I don't like her and she's better at it than me so I need to criticize her to make myself feel better."

"Oh, of course!" Ross said matter-of-factly.

"I like what you did here though," said Turk watching a ridiculous scene where his brother was contorting his face trying to, apparently, convey emotion.

"Right! For a second, I really felt like I was about to crash in this machine. Maybe that's what the problem is, once we'll be in costumes with the set built and all, it'll be easier to get into character, I think. Let's try to find older movies. Stop clicking on everything, you're going to break it!" said Ross tapping on his brother's hand. "See, you messed it up. This is not a movie, it's just a record of the cameras by the roundhouse so you're just going to be seeing a whole lot of nothing. OK, that's better, OK, I think we just found a great one, I believe this is supposed to be a girl but it really is Artea with a wig and a dress jumping from that building. That's amazing! OK, but that's not helping our acting and we do need to improve, brother! Let's focus."

They kept on clicking in and out of different files trying to find a video to inspire them.

"Oh, look at that one when they were a lot younger. This movie must be like 10 years old or something. I wish we had movies of us, this way we would have memories of our childhood and of our parents. Don't you think they got the coolest village?"

"Well, at least we didn't get the shittiest one," said Ross.

"Robin?"

"Err, duh?"

"Yeah you're right, I mean Adimen is cool but a whole village of Adimens would be tough," said Turk trying to picture the scene.

"We look better in Robat," said Ross trying to point out Robat's good sides.

"Don't forget they have Artea and we have Tom!"

"Good point!" said Ross amused.

⚏⚎

Probably about that same time, but who can tell with those people, they're everywhere. . .

"So, is Adimen always this bossy?" asked James while gluing two slates of wood together.

"Oh, that? That's nothing. She can be a bit of a know-it-all but the truth is she really is smart and she is a great person, in small quantities," said Tom smiling. "That's kind of annoying that we can't do our design the way we want it," said Tom changing topic.

"It actually went kind of well. Basically, Indarra and Phil's job and our jobs are somehow very similar and very different at the same time, know what I mean? On one hand, they give us design restrictions but if we complain they will tell us that if we're not happy, they're going to CGI the crap out of it because CGI has no limits. However, it is time-consuming and makes everything look a little bit too perfect so we prefer to work with practical elements as much as possible. If we have to sink one of those water machines, then we like to do it real time, live, with minimal CGI and have the actors experience the whole thing for real. You get better acting that way. Of course, we can't make rooms float in the air, but you would be surprised what can be achieved with camera angles. The eye can easily be tricked!"

"This is amazing, you know, we don't do things like this where I'm from."

"Really? What do you guys do there?"

"Who the hell knows but we sweat a lot! Always competing at this and that . . ."

"And you lose a lot?" asked James as if he was just describing something which he hadn't had time yet to make up his opinion on whether it was a good or a bad thing.

"And . . . I lose a lot," said Tom smiling. "Indarra is really good though, she always had it in her, you know at, err, being good at everything."

"Yeah, she seems like she has a wide variety of skills. Are you excited to return home tomorrow?" asked James.

"No, honestly, if I could be selfish, I would never return, I would just stay here and be happy till the end. I have no one left I care about there. I came with my friends here, made a new one on the way, and a whole lot more here, plus my family is gone so . . . honestly, I am doing it because they all wanna go back or think it's the right thing to do, but I don't really feel like it."

"You will be back, don't worry, people will just go wherever they feel like, right? That's the whole point of this adventure!"

After a long day working on the new movie together, they were all happy to meet at dinner and share their experience of the day, above all Adimen who obviously had much to say about it.

"So I told James, of course, this design seems great, but it needs to be feasible. After all, floating objects answer to laws we can't ignore. Of course, we can use other forces if we're well-versed in that topic, but then we can't ignore material restrictions and we can't possibly build a 70,000-ton machine I told him."

"Well, of course not!" said Turk mocking Adimen who did not notice.

"Oh, and I put together something really useful for the future – hydrofluoric acid. It's very simple to make if you have the formula, see, it could melt your face off in an instant." She handled the plastic bottle clumsily over the table scaring everyone. "It dissolves metal, so if we wanted to sink one of the floating machines, we would just have to pour it over the nails mid-shoot and bang, we could sink it live! Give me your fork, Turk!" ordered Adimen, gesturing towards him.

"But how will I eat then?" asked Turk looking at his food with concern.

"Oh, don't be such a baby, I'll just do the tip!" She poured a couple drops on the fork and a hole appeared in it to everyone's amazement!

"What if it burnt through the bottle?" asked Indarra.

"It does not dissolve plastic, you silly berry!" Adimen rolled her eyes as if someone was trying to stick their fingers in boiling water and had to be told not to.

"Yes, but what if the cap came off?" asked Indarra again.

"Then I would probably try to reach for water in a moment of despair because of the tremendous pain of skin, flesh, muscles, and nerves being dissolved on my leg, but you should not let me as water would only make it worse and spread the burn. So please think of restraining me if this happens."

She continued eating her food as everyone looked at her in a mixture of fear and amazement.

"So," started Artea, "is everyone happy with their first day in the movie industry? Any other stories that don't involve melting legs off with acid?"

"Well, I got to build the first floating machine!" said Tom excitedly. "It looks awesome and let me tell you something, no one is sticking acid on my baby's nails!"

"Yeah, wait till Adimonic uses her superpowers and makes thousands of liters of water gush into your beautiful baby," laughed Turk.

"Oh, good job, Tom!" said Indarra in an overly motherly tone as if a toddler had just brought her a wooden stick he had found on the ground. She realized right away, made a face, and went on. "I need new elbows. Artea made me jump off that roof for hours and let's just say that the fall and roll on your side thing is easier in theory, above all when you have bones in your body . . . but it was fun and I really needed the thrill."

Phil was overly excited about the trip the day after and did not seem to know what outfit would be appropriate to meet new people. Considering he was in team Adimen, this should not have been his first concern.

"Alright, everyone, tomorrow is a big day and we have a long walk ahead of us so we should all go to sleep really early," declared Indarra bossily.

Everyone wished everyone else a good night and retreated to their respective bungalows.

Indarra turned to Artea during this and said, "Meet me in my bungalow in an hour."

Artea walked back to his place; he had left his beach-front bungalow the day the First Generation disappeared to move as far away from the water as possible. What he did not know was that the water was going to bring him, what I hope, is the comfort and happiness he had been looking for for a very long time.

⁂

"Mom, I don't see why I can't get flippers. You work at the roundhouse so you can easily get a pair. I wanna learn how to fish and swim at the bottom of the lagoon," said Artea.

"You will do as you are told and stop bothering me. Why can't you be like your brother? Look at him," and she pointed

at his little brother as if he was a pile of gold sitting by a pile of poop. "He's three years younger and so much better than you at everything already, you should be ashamed of yourself," and she hit him across the face.

Artea fell on the floor and a few drops of blood ran from his forehead. Teddy was only seven but ran to his brother crying, begging their mother to stop. She had not planned on hitting him again anyway so she just went back to what she was doing and the two brothers ended up alone on the floor of their parents' room.

"Please, Artea, please, do what mom tells you or she will hit you again," begged little Teddy.

"I don't care anymore, one day I will walk up the mountain and leave forever. She loves you anyway so you'll be fine."

"Please don't leave me alone!" Little Teddy grabbed Artea and started sobbing harder in his brother's neck.

After a while, they worked on little Teddy's sand-construction building ability, which was their mother's morning request. She thought little Teddy was extremely talented at this too and his brother should assist him. Regardless of the fact that Artea was three years his elder, he lacked any talent, according to their mother. They stayed at the beach for a while. Artea loved spending time with his baby brother even though making sandcastles was not really his thing. They used very wet sand to design features on the roofs. The whole thing was pretty impressive, they managed to reproduce the whole village in detail.

"Teddy, how about I let you finish the fountain and I'll be back in a few minutes. If you see mom, tell her I am in the bathroom."

Artea walked to the left side of the village and snuck up the road to the roundhouse. He could hear voices from the kitchen on the other side. He walked around the roundhouse and put his ear against the door to make sure nobody was in there, especially his mom. His idea was to go inside and get flippers. He did not know how but he knew that's where they would come from. Hearing no noise, he put his hand on the knob and the door swung open. His mother was there and the blow that followed was so hard it actually knocked him out for a few seconds. When he opened his eyes and regained consciousness, his ears were ringing. He tried to get up, pressing his hands against his ears in a desperate attempt to stop the noise ringing in his ears. However, then he realized it was not in his ears but coming from within the ground, and it was shaking. He got up to his feet and his mother's petrified and uncomprehending eyes narrowed. The sound seemed to come from the beach, but all he could see were the roofs and palm trees until it sounded like something had punched the walls and the palm trees bent and disappeared behind the roofs.

Indarra was now back in her bungalow, more determined than ever to solve the roundhouse mystery. She had no idea what she would find behind that door, but she had to find out. Besides, she figured they would most probably get things they would need in the future such as medicines. She couldn't stay still and paced around the room like a maniac until finally, she heard a knock on the door. She opened it without asking who it was and let the handsome man into her room.

"Nobody saw you come here?" asked Indarra feeling important.

"Hmm, I don't think so," said Artea, not feeling as much in the shoes of a spy.

"Alright, let's just head straight there now. I don't wanna use any main roads, which means no beach and no Main Street," commanded Indarra.

They walked outside and went left twice to move away from the beach and then turned right towards the East Road. They moved along very quietly. Every once in a while, Indarra turned back towards Artea to remind him to be quiet, even though he was walking with a much lighter step than her. Once they reached the East Road, they made a left towards the back of the village. They made it to the barn where they heard voices. It seemed like Tatiana was still in there and they wondered if she was sleeping there? They walked along the fields all the way to West Road and made a left. They walked down and there it was, the roundhouse, the place everyone had ignored for so long. But then again, they did not really see it this way, it was not the only place they had been prohibited from visiting, this being just a room, no wonder it had taken them this long to build up the curiosity to go inside and break the rules. They were both standing by the door and somehow it seemed even more challenging than stepping on the mountain for the first time. Indarra put her hand on the knob, twisted it, and pushed. The excitement died out pretty quickly when nothing happened and they realized it was locked.

"Yeah . . . I had a feeling it wouldn't be that easy. Ideas?" asked Indarra.

"Maybe we could try kicking it?" said Artea casually.

"How about I start kicking your head?" Indarra slowly turned her head towards Artea and, her face went from something freaky to a funny face and they both laughed. "Jokes aside," she went on, "I don't think kicking it is the way to go, to be honest. First, it's a very big door and on top of this, we are trying to be discreet and I don't think that a repeated banging noise would be a great idea."

"Maybe we should try to get in from the roof. If we started deconstructing the roof one piece at a time we would maybe get in."

"Remind me to ask Adimen instead of you next time I go on a night mission." Indarra elbowed him in the belly a little harder than intended.

"Well, say all you want, if I really wanted I could kick that door down but I can't really see Adimen do it, or you for that matter."

"Mister, you did not just say that. I am strong! I am really strong!"

"Really? Yeah, you're strong but—"

Artea did not get to finish his sentence.

"My good man, I believe you have just been challenged to a game of arm wrestling." Indarra took on an impressive posture flexing her biceps.

"You're right, Adimen would probably be better at this, you get pulled out of focus too easily," said Artea raising an eyebrow in defiance.

"Damn you're lucky you're pretty, Artea. I will spare you the shame of losing against me at arm wrestling." She started fiddling with the lock then looked back at him and added, "This time only!" She smiled, winked, and then focused on the door again. "OK, we're not getting in like this and I don't think we can discreetly start deconstructing a building in the middle of the night. It has no windows so the door is probably where we wanna focus our attention. The only thing that has locks where I am from is the barn but they are much simpler and meant to keep the animals in their fences."

"Well, maybe we could ask—" but Artea once again did not get to finish his sentence.

"Artea, you just wanna receive tough love from me don't you." She laughed. "We're not asking Tatiana if she can help us bust that lock, but I can think of someone else who already did!"

"What do you mean?" asked Artea surprised.

"Well, it annoys me to admit it, but the one person we joked about earlier really is the person who can get us into that room, only she doesn't need to know about it."

"Adimen?"

"The one and only!"

"The acid!" declared Artea triumphantly.

"Yep, the acid. She said it could melt basically anything but plastic."

"She also said it could melt flesh," said Artea making a disgusted face.

"Well, let's not use it as mouthwash and we should be OK," said Indarra.

"OK, but you said we could do it without her, you have the recipe?"

⚒

Two minutes later at Adimen's . . .

"Hey there, your hair looks crazy!" said Indarra making one of her crazy facial expressions. "So, we need your acid."

"What for?" asked Adimen suddenly truly waking up.

"Well, we wanna break into the roundhouse and we need the acid to melt the lock, so, we need it!"

"Wait! What? Hang on!"

They spoke for a few minutes and Adimen had her own epiphany about the roundhouse and decided to go with them. Having clumsy Adimen deal with acid after being awakened in the middle of the night was not really reassuring, but desperate times called for desperate measures, even if that meant the nastiest splash back in the history of Robart.

"I can't see anything! Go get me light," said Adimen.

"Light? As in you want me to get you light from somewhere and carefully carry it in my hands over here for you to see?" asked Indarra confused.

"Go and get matches from the kitchen, people!"

Indarra came back with the matches and Adimen started pouring the liquid carefully on the lock. Each time she poured it, it would start smoking and smelled funny, but nothing happened.

"It's not working, Adimen!" said Indarra feeling impatient. "Are you sure you're pouring it right?"

"Do you know of many different ways to pour?"

"Well, aim better or we're gonna run out of that—"

At that moment, they heard something fall on the other side of the door and it opened slightly.

Adimen turned to her friends with her eyes wide open, probably surprised that it actually worked! She jerked her arm towards the door to open it. At first, they couldn't see anything as the room was so bright while it was dark outside. When their sight adjusted to the light, they finally were able to see inside.

"Well, I must say, this is slightly underwhelming," said Adimen looking around the empty room.

They all entered the windowless space of the roundhouse.

"What the heck! It just can't be, there has to be something here, there just has to be!" said Indarra in a trembling voice, grabbing at Adimen's arm as if she hoped she would somehow make things happen. "Adimen, I don't understand. Who are we? Who are they? Why are they doing this to us?" she was hysterical. After a while, she sat down against one of the walls.

Artea and Adimen were also surprised there was nothing to find inside the roundhouse but they were not as bothered. To some extent, they probably didn't want or need the room to have anything in it. For Indarra, it was a different story as she was the only one who had actually gone through the whole discovery step by step. To think of it, Tom did too, but he was not there at that moment and Indarra had done the heavy lifting all along.

"I don't care if they're traitors and abandoned us," she was crying now. "I just need to know, as freaking shitty as the truth can get, I need it, please!" she said squeezing Adimen's arm with even more strength.

After a while, she resumed breathing at a normal pace again. The other two sat down next to her, silently comforting her. They stared at the bare grey walls for a while, from time to time they would tuck their legs under their butt, then they would stretch them, desperately trying to find a comfortable position. Then, Artea got to his feet and walked around the room, stopping at the obvious trap door, which somehow hadn't registered to them until now. He grabbed the handle, pulled, and the gigantic door swung open with a bang. Artea looked back at the girls as if he hadn't understood what he had just done and wanted to see if his action received a positive or negative reaction. Adimen and Indarra finally got to their feet and walked over to him. They all stared at the stairs leading down from the trap door. They seemed to go on forever.

"Where does this go?" asked Artea, not to anyone in particular.

"Guys, I'll go down first. There's no need for all of us to go and besides, someone needs to look out so no one sees we're here. I'll explore and once I know it's safe, we'll all go together."

"Are you—" Artea began but Indarra interrupted him.

"I'm not asking you to let me be brave; I'm asking you for a favor, an unreasonable favor. You all deserve to know what happened to your families, who you are, and what this place is. Right now, at least for the next 20 minutes, I need to do this alone; I need to deal with this alone. Will you please let me be selfish for a little bit? It means everything to me."

I don't think she knew if she was lying to protect them or if she really meant it. It was probably a little bit of both. Either way, it worked.

"Indarra, of course, after all you've been through," said Adimen. "I mean, without you, we wouldn't be here. I would still be alone in that big house trying to figure this all out from my books. We'll stay and keep a look out and wait until you're ready to share what you find."

"Scream, pretty girl if anything happens, OK?" Artea gave her an awkward tap on the back.

Indarra nodded and took a first step. It took her at least five minutes to reach the bottom of the stairs that plunged straight down towards the heart of the island. At the end of what must have been a 500-meter straight slope, she slowed down. She was now a little worried. Was knowing really better? Maybe it was actually better to guess. However, she hadn't gone this far to stop now. She walked the last few steps, which led to a long corridor. Just like the stairs, the corridor was well lit. It had fluorescent lights on both the green walls and the ceiling. The floor was made of a material that muffled the sound of her steps. It was green too but covered in black marks. After a few minutes, she could finally see the end of the corridor. At its end, she found a huge round room. To the right of this room, from where she was standing, there was a sign pointing towards another corridor that said 'ROBIN', while to the left another sign said 'ROBAT', her home. Next to the corridor to Robat was another corridor, but this one went deeper into the ground. Next to that corridor was a door with neither a lock or a knob. She tried to push it, but nothing happened. She decided she'd look into it later and headed towards the only corridor that didn't have a sign. She was neither cautious nor scared as there was nothing to be scared of. She walked for 15 minutes and made it to a staircase , it wasn't a slope like the one going down from Robart but an actual staircase going straight up. There was another very large door without a knob or a lock next to it but she ignored it again and went up the stairs. Indarra was exhausted by the time she made it up, as there were at least 30 flights of stairs. After so much walking, her excitement had become less intense to the point she was almost bored and wished Adimen and Artea had come with her. The last flight of stairs led to a room with a single large sliding door. She could hear a commotion beyond the walls of the room, but it was not loud enough to distract her from what she saw scribbled on the wall by the sliding door: 'INDARRA, GO BACK! FORGIVE ME. M.'

"They're alive," whispered Indarra, feeling the words under her fingers. Everything started shaking around her and pulled her from her reverie. She looked around, trying to get hold of something to find her balance. She reached for the huge door, slid it open, and walked out into the open. The light from the wall of searchlights on her right was so strong she couldn't do anything but protect her face with her arms. The noise around her and those lights made her lose all her senses. She was so confused she almost fell over. After a few seconds, she turned her back to the lights and saw they pointed towards the Robat beach. She was standing in the middle of the ocean, right in front of the 'star' she used to see from her village, day and night. She walked around the searchlights to the other side of the platform where she wouldn't be blinded by the light and saw what, to her, looked like a huge building moving away in the water. As the massive boat sailed away, she read the letters 'R.O.B' on its stern.

"Moooom!" Indarra yelled at the boat and ran to the edge of the platform. She jumped in the water and tried to swim to the boat, forgetting all about the sharks. When she realized she could not catch the boat, she stopped and looked around her, trying to catch her breath. That is when she remembered the sharks, only there weren't any. She could see their fins over by the coral reef, but none were near her although they would have swum towards her by now if they could. She swam slowly towards the coral reef, watching their fins as she grew closer. However, they did not approach her even though they were only a few meters away now. She was scared but couldn't stop herself swimming closer and closer until she banged against something solid in the water. She screamed thinking one of the sharks had grabbed her but it was hard and cold – a metal bar, floating on the surface of the ocean. She swam underwater and saw a net running all the way down to the bottom. The sharks were actually trapped between the reef and a net, which was less than 500 meters from the reef. This whole time, if they'd only had a boat, they could have sailed those 500 meters past the sharks. What's more, they weren't even trying to get her through the net. They were just minding their own business, swimming around, probably waiting for death to free them from their prison. She started swimming back to the platform when she saw a light appear in the sky.

Artea and Adimen were still standing behind the roundhouse, waiting for Indarra as they tried to guess what might be hidden beyond the trapdoor.

Suddenly, Artea shouted, "Stop!"

"What?" asked Adimen.

"Don't you hear it?"

"Hear what?"

"Hush, listen!" commanded Artea holding his index finger up for Adimen to be quiet.

They heard a humming noise that seemed to echo around them. It was getting louder and louder every second. They looked around, trying to understand where the noise came from. Adimen was curious what the noise could be but she saw the fear in Artea's eyes.

"We should never have done that, oh no! I killed him and it's happening again. Go hide! Go up to the top of the forum!" screamed Artea in absolute panic.

They ran to the top of the building and waited for the wave to hit, only, the water was perfectly calm.

"Look at that star," said Adimen. "It's moving towards us."

The light was getting more and more intense and the noise was so loud they actually had to cover their ears until they saw flight F0981 crash into the sea right behind the reef and smash into it. They saw the sharks swim around it. It took them a couple of minutes before they heard the screams over the noise of the explosions, the waves, and the absolute chaos unraveling before their eyes. They were petrified and could not understand what they were seeing. There was debris everywhere and it seemed like the ocean was on fire.

"Do you see that?" asked Artea pointing at something that seemed like nothing in particular to Adimen. "There's a shadow, over there, standing on the reef. I think I see someone."

The shadow dove into the water and started swimming towards the beach. As they ran down the stairs towards the ocean, other people started to walk out of their bungalows wondering what the noise was.

Artea ran as fast as he could into the water as if it was air. The bay had filled with all sorts of debris as the belly of the plane spilled food trays, suitcases, and bodies . . . Right before he made it to the struggling body, he brushed the 2015 copy of the airline magazine with his hand. As he pushed it away, the magazine opened to the perfume page. Artea grabbed the body and dragged it to shore. When he finally hauled it out of the water, he fell onto his back.

"Hello, hi, are you alright?" asked Artea, struggling to sit up with the weight of my body on top of his.

And I said, "What's this island?" to which Artea replied, "What's an island?"

To be continued . . .

Printed in Poland
by Amazon Fulfillment
Poland Sp. z o.o., Wrocław

22883455R00163